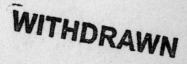

Liars

P.J. Petersen

2.00

SCHOLASTIC INC.
New York Toronto London Auckland Sydney

ISBN 0-590-25629-7

12 11 10 9 8 7 6 5 4 3 2   5 6 7 8 9/9

Printed in the U.S.A.   01

First Scholastic printing, October 1994

For Ivy Ruckman

WITHDRAWN

One

When I say I'm from Alder Creek, everybody says, "Where's that?" Except for one wise guy who said, "That's too bad."

The wise guy had a point though. My friend Marty McNabb says the biggest thrills in Alder Creek are watching the paint peel off the houses and listening to the cars rust. People move here for peace and quiet, he says, then move away when they've had all the peace and quiet they can stand.

Alder Creek is in California, but don't start thinking about Hollywood and surfers. The old sign on the Alder Creek Store used to say LOS ANGELES—693 MILES, but somebody scratched out the 693 and wrote in 1 MILLION. Either way, you get the idea.

If you're in Alder Creek and you need a Big Mac or a hospital, you'd better not need them too bad. It's a two-hour drive to the town of Yreka, most of it over roads that aren't wide enough for two cars.

We are smack in the middle of nowhere and too small to show up on a map. Downtown Alder Creek is one store with a gas pump outside and the post office in a back corner. The official population is two hundred, but that count was taken before the lumber mill closed. These days you'd have to throw in all the dogs to get two hundred. Maybe some cats too.

My family moved to Alder Creek when I was in fifth grade, so I'm finishing my fourth year with the same teacher in the same one-room school. (Actually, the school has two rooms, but we use the other room for storage and the library.) Our teacher, Mr. Harrison, isn't a bad guy, but after four years I've heard all his jokes—at least twenty times.

Marty invented two words that cover everything about school—SOT and MOTSOT (*Same Old Thing* and *More Of The Same Old Thing*). Day after boring day, we were dying for some kind of change. We didn't care what, just so it was different.

Be careful what you wish for. Your wish might come true.

The whole crazy business started on a Friday, G-Day minus forty-four. (Forty-four school days until graduation.) As usual, the whole Alder Creek Elementary School—all sixteen of us—had piled on the rickety bus for a Friday afternoon field trip. And, as usual, Marty and I were slumped down in the backseat, where Mr. Harrison couldn't see us in the mirror. Mr. Harrison, you see, isn't just the teacher. He also drives the bus, runs the library, and cleans the floors—or makes us clean them.

Everybody else on the bus was singing "The Happy Wanderer," which has to be the second worst song in the world. The worst is "Row, Row, Row Your Boat," and that was coming next.

Our first stop of the afternoon was at Amy Ricketts's place. Amy's ugly orange-striped alley cat had had seven ugly orange-striped kittens. Each of the little kids got a kitty to hold, and Amy's mother kept telling us to ask our parents if we could keep one. Good luck.

We made a quick stop at Guido Cavalo's greenhouse so that the middle graders could measure the plants for their science project. Then we headed for the Caldwell place to watch Uncle Gene Gaither do water witching.

We weren't supposed to call it water witching though. It was dowsing. Last fall, a couple of the mothers had made a big fuss about our Halloween party. They thought it was devil worship or something. And Mr. Harrison didn't want to stir up that hornets' nest again with talk about witching. So it was dowsing, which sounded a lot more boring.

Whatever you called it, I didn't believe in it. To me, it was another one of Uncle Gene's crazy notions, like wearing garlic to keep away cold germs and searching for lost mines.

Marty wasn't so sure. "Let's see how it works," he said. "Mr. Harrison said Uncle Gene used to do it a lot, and he's never had a dry well."

"I asked Dad about that," I told him. "He said it'd be almost impossible to drill a well around here and *not* hit water."

Marty smiled and looked away. That drove me crazy. He'd never argue, even if he knew he was right. I sometimes felt like a bully, which didn't make sense. He was six inches taller than I was and forty pounds heavier. But he was always the one to give in.

"You believe in that stuff, don't you?" I asked. "You actually believe Uncle Gene can find water with a stupid stick."

Marty shrugged. "It's possible."

"Anything's possible," I said. "It's possible we could have an earthquake right now, but—"

Marty punched my arm. "Take it easy, dude. I still believe in Santa Claus too."

"All right," Mr. Harrison called. "Let's do 'Row, Row, Row Your Boat.' And we'll let the eighth grade start."

The little kids cheered, of course. Marty and I *were* the eighth grade.

"Let the seventh grade start," I yelled. Carmen Williams, sitting in the seat in front of us, was the only seventh grader.

"I'll help you get started," Carmen said. "That way, I don't have to listen to you sing." So the three of us started out the round, and everybody else joined in when their turn came. I'd sung that dumb song at least five hundred times in the past four years. That was Alder Creek—SOT and MOTSOT.

But things were about to change.

The road up to the pasture was too steep for the old bus, so Mr. Harrison parked at a wide spot and led us up the hill. We hadn't gone ten steps before the little kids were yelling, "I'm tired, I'm tired." As usual, they wanted piggyback rides.

So, as usual, I carried Bobby Keck, the littlest boy. Aurelia Lopez (the only sixth grader) and Carmen carried the two smallest girls. Mr. Harrison and Marty carried some of the bigger kids, dumping them off every little while to give somebody else a turn.

Uncle Gene was sitting in the grass by the pasture gate. His straw hat was tipped down to shade his eyes. With his red face and his white beard, he looks like a skinny Santa Claus. "You kids are too late," he called. "I've already figured out where the well should go."

"No! No!" the little ones shouted.

Uncle Gene laughed and used the gate to pull himself up. "You don't want me to work overtime, do you?"

"Yes!" they yelled.

Uncle Gene brushed off his old jeans and walked toward us. "Okay, kids, who wants to shake my hand, and who wants to pat my beard?"

"Beard! Beard!" the little kids yelled, the way they always did.

The little kids filed past him, rubbing their grubby hands on his long white beard. "Where's Leonard?" Amy Ricketts asked him. Leonard was Uncle Gene's old llama.

"That lazy thing," Uncle Gene said. "I left him home today."

The little kids all went "Aww," but they were just as happy. Leonard acted friendly enough, but then he'd spit without any warning, aiming for your face. Llama spit is even worse than you think—thick and green and smelly. Uncle Gene always said it wasn't Leonard's fault, that he'd been teased when he was little. But that didn't help much when you got a face full of green spit.

Out in the pasture, Uncle Gene showed us his forked stick.

"I just cut this today," he said. "Plain old willow stick. But it told me right where the best water is." He used the stick to scratch the back of his neck. "Who wants to try it?"

And, of course, the little ones all waved their hands in the air and yelled, "Me! Me!"

Marty and Carmen and I stayed back out of the way while all the kids went charging around the field with the stick. When everybody else had done it, including Mr. Harrison, Carmen gave it a try. She came back shaking her head. "I knew I wasn't a witch."

Marty took the stick and started across the field, but he turned back after about thirty feet. "I didn't find water," he said, scraping his foot on the grass. "But I found something else. Stepped right in the middle of it." He handed Uncle Gene the stick. "What's it supposed to do?"

Uncle Gene laughed. "You'd know it if it did it." Then he turned to me. "Come on, boy."

"That's okay," I said.

"Come on, Sam," the little ones yelled.

"We all tried it," Carmen said.

So I took the stick and let Uncle Gene fix my hands on it. "Now what?" I asked.

"Just go for a stroll," Uncle Gene said.

I felt stupid walking along with the stick in the air. "I'm glad nobody has a camera," I said.

"Watch out," Marty said. "You're about to step in the same stuff I did."

I cut to the left. "Can I stop now?" I asked.

Then the stick started to twist in my hands. I grabbed it tight, trying to hold it steady. But the point dipped toward the ground. It was like holding a fishing pole with a big trout on the line.

"He's faking," somebody yelled.

I backed up a few steps, and the point of the stick rose toward the sky. Carmen came running toward me. "Was that real? Did it work?"

"This is crazy," I said.

"Keep walking," Uncle Gene called.

I moved forward and felt the stick twisting. I took one more step, and the point sank to the ground. Then it bobbed up and down like a chicken drinking water. "I can't hold it still," I told Carmen.

Behind me, Uncle Gene was cackling. "I think that boy's got it."

Marty started laughing. "Come on, Sam," he yelled. "You don't believe in that stuff, do you?"

"What's it feel like?" Carmen asked me.

"Like a magnet," I said.

By then, the other kids were all around me. "Try it with him," Uncle Gene told Carmen. He had us hold hands and put our free hands on the stick. When we walked forward, the stick dipped, just the way it had before.

"Wow!" Carmen shouted. "This is wild!"

Then everybody had to try it with me. It worked better with some kids than others, but they all got the feeling. Some of them still thought I was faking it though.

When everybody'd had a turn, Uncle Gene came over and put his hand on my shoulder. "Before you go, boy, I want you to take a run over the pasture. Let's see what you find."

"Stand back, ladies and gentlemen," Carmen shouted,

using her fist like a microphone. "It's time for the Water-Witching Olympics."

I picked up the stick, and everybody cheered. It felt good to be star of the show, even if it wasn't a very big show.

The stick twitched when I passed over my old spot. I kept walking, and the twitching slowed. "He's going forward," Carmen announced. "He's still looking."

A little farther on, I could feel the pull again. "Something here," I said. "Not so strong."

"That's right, boy," Uncle Gene said.

I moved around the meadow for a while without getting much. A couple of the boys started wrestling in the grass. "Try it to your right," Uncle Gene called.

Pretty soon the stick was bobbing up and down. "It's all over the place." Just then I felt a surge through my elbows and wrists. The stick spun in my hand, and the point jabbed at the ground. "This is the granddaddy!" I yelled.

Uncle Gene was laughing again. "Circle around there, boy. Figure out where the pull's the strongest."

I backed up, then crisscrossed the area. The palms of my hands got sore from the branch twisting. "Right here," I said finally. "It's strongest right here."

"Keep your stick on the spot," Uncle Gene called. "Then look around. You see something?"

I looked down at the grass and weeds. "No."

"Look close," Uncle Gene said. "See something white?"

Then I saw it—a matchbook cover about six inches from my stick. "A matchbook," I said.

Uncle Gene let out a cackle. "Come on, kids. Take a look at this."

They all came running up to me. When Uncle Gene got there, he turned to Carmen. "Let's have this smart young lady pick up the matchbook."

Carmen crossed her eyes and stuck out her tongue. Then she reached for the matchbook. "It's stuck," she said.

"I put a nail through it," Uncle Gene said. "Just open the cover." Carmen squatted and opened the cover of the matchbook. "Now read what it says."

Carmen glanced down, then looked up at Uncle Gene. Then she turned my way. "It says, 'Dig here.'"

Uncle Gene let out another cackle.

TWO

"That's the way things go," Marty said as we walked back to the bus. "You go out there and find out you have magical powers, and I go out and step in a llama pie."

"That was a plain old cow pie," I said. "And dowsing isn't magic." I still had the forked stick with me. Uncle Gene said any forked stick would work, but I wanted to keep that one.

"If it's not magic, what is it?"

I shrugged. "It's just something that's there. Like electricity."

"Electricity's magic to me," Marty said.

Dr. Vincent's Range Rover was parked behind the bus. Dr. Vincent was down in the ditch, picking up cans. He was wearing his hiking outfit—khaki shirt and shorts with a Smokey-the-Bear hat. As usual, he had his leather knapsack and his stainless steel walking stick.

"Get ready for the litter lecture," Marty said.

Seeing Dr. Vincent on our field trip was MOTSOT. He showed up anytime something was happening around Alder

Creek. He would have been mayor of the town if we'd had a mayor. He was chairman of the school board and chief of the volunteer fire department. He wasn't a medical doctor—his doctor's degree was in biology—but he knew first aid. Which made him the closest thing we had to a doctor anyway.

Dr. Vincent was also the only man in Alder Creek who wore shorts and the only famous person I knew. He wrote nature books, big books full of pictures. We had a whole shelf of them at school, and Mr. Lopez had some for sale at the Alder Creek Store.

Billy Cavalo ran down the hill toward him. "Hi, Dr. Vincent. Sam's a water witch. And we all did it with him."

Dr. Vincent smiled and nodded and waved us in close. When we'd formed a half-circle around him, he said, "Boys and girls, I want to warn all of you about dowsing. And that's the proper name—dowsing. As interesting as it may seem, it has no basis in scientific fact."

Uncle Gene snorted. "It works—that's all I know."

Dr. Vincent went on about water tables and university studies. An hour earlier I would have been right with him. Now I had the stick in my hand, and I was getting little twitches right where we stood.

Just when the lecture seemed to be over, Dr. Vincent leaned his shiny walking stick against the bus and opened his knapsack. "Look inside, boys and girls," he said, holding it in front of each of us. "It's a shame and a disgrace." The knapsack was full of cans and bottles and tangles of fishing line. "I picked up all this trash right around here."

"It's the city people," Uncle Gene said. "They're the ones that mess things up."

"It's everybody," Dr. Vincent said. He set down the knap-sack and gave us his lecture about litter. I looked over and saw Marty mouthing the words.

Even with his boring lectures, I liked Dr. Vincent. He was always showing up at school with something new—an empty hornets' nest, a trapdoor spider, a videotape he'd made of mountain goats. And he'd locate things like beaver dams or ground squirrel colonies for our field trips.

So we all stood there and pretended to listen. I noticed Mr. Harrison checking his watch. Uncle Gene was the only one who really got into it. He kept muttering "That's right" and "You betcha" the whole time.

When Dr. Vincent finally finished and asked for questions, Bobby Keck was the only one to raise his hand. Dr. Vincent smiled at him. "Yes, young man?"

Bobby pointed at Dr. Vincent's bare legs and asked, "Don't your knees ever get cold?"

Mr. Harrison stopped the bus beside the Alder Creek Store. "Uncle Gene has offered to buy ice cream bars for everybody," he called. "What do we say?"

"Thank you, Uncle Gene," the little ones yelled.

"Mr. Harrison," Jenny Cavalo shouted, "Billy can't have an ice cream bar."

Billy muttered something.

"Mr. Harrison," Jenny shouted again, "Billy called me a dirty name."

Mr. Harrison opened the door of the bus. "We'll let Car-men and Aurelia buy the ice cream. And they can get a banana for Billy. The rest of you can get out, but don't go inside the store."

"Good," I said. "At least we don't have to mess with Luther."

Luther was a third grader with the fastest hands in the world. One trip down the aisle, and he had his shirt stuffed with candy bars and his socks full of bubble gum. Whenever Mr. Lopez invited the school to come and see something at the store, Marty and I had to hold Luther's hands the whole time.

"You must be feeling rich today, Uncle Gene," Marty said when we climbed off the bus.

"Made me a hundred dollars yesterday," Uncle Gene said in a whisper that could have been heard a mile away.

"What did you do?" I asked him. "Sell your place?"

"Ask me next week," Uncle Gene said. "I can't tell you right now."

"Okay," Marty said.

But I'm not like Marty. Curious, nosy—I don't care what you call it. If there's a secret, I want to know it. Right now. "Come on," I said. "You can tell us."

He took off his hat and wiped his bald head with his shirt-sleeve. "I'm gonna use the whole hundred for groceries. Gonna load up Leonard and go on a real hunt for that mine."

"Where'd you get the hundred dollars?" I broke in. If he got going on the Barkley Mine, we'd never hear about anything else.

Everybody in Alder Creek knew about the Barkley Mine, but Uncle Gene was probably the only one who believed in it.

According to the old stories, a miner named Barkley rode into Yreka with sacks full of gold. He said he'd just started working this mine over by Alder Creek. And he died right in the Wells Fargo office. Or he got shot in a card game that night. Or he got thrown by a horse and broke his neck. Every story was different. But all the stories had the important thing—the hidden gold mine waiting for somebody to find it and get filthy rich.

Uncle Gene planned to be that somebody. He'd spent years going through papers collected by the county historical society, and he had photocopies of old journals and scrawled-out maps. He spent most of his time poking around empty gullies and brushy canyons, looking for that hidden mine shaft. "With a full pack on Leonard," he told us, "we can stay out two, three weeks. Do nothing but look."

"Come on, Uncle Gene," I said. "Where'd you get a hundred bucks? Marty and I won't tell anybody. I swear it."

He took us around to the front of the bus. "Well, see," he said, looking back over his shoulder, "I ran across a patch of marijuana out there. Just new planted. Up one of those skinny canyons by Fisher Peak."

"Really?" I said.

Uncle Gene checked over his shoulder again. "You know what that means, don't you? A hundred dollars reward. Minimum."

"Maybe," Marty said.

"I know what you mean," Uncle Gene said. "But I didn't take no chances this time. They won't cheat me again."

I knew what was coming. I'd heard the story almost as often as I'd heard the litter lecture.

But Uncle Gene gave it to us again. "They cheated me two years ago. Sheriff said what I found was just a couple of plants, not a real patch. What could I say? It was all gone by then."

"That stinks," I said, edging away.

"That's when I bought me that Polaroid camera," Uncle Gene went on. "I don't go nowhere without sticking it in my pack. So this time, when I found that stuff, I took pictures of everything. A whole roll. Let him try and say I didn't find no patch this time." He laughed and smacked the bus radiator with the back of his hand. "So tomorrow Deputy Bates is bringing out horses, and I'll take him up there. Then Sunday I'll get my groceries. And Monday morning I'll head out. I know where I went wrong before. I put these maps together, see, and I think there used to be a trail—"

"We'd better get our ice cream before it melts," Marty said. "Good luck out there."

"I got me a feeling this is the time," Uncle Gene said.

Aurelia and Carmen handed out the ice cream bars. Right away Billy Cavalo traded his banana to Bobby Keck for an ice cream, then downed the ice cream before his sister caught on.

When Carmen handed me an ice cream bar, she whispered, "They're getting a new shipment of videos this afternoon."

Whenever new videos came in, there was always a mad rush. The mountains surrounding Alder Creek were so high that only people with satellite dishes could watch TV. The rest of us had VCRs. We rented movies from the store and borrowed tapes from Mr. Harrison's school collection.

Usually I was first in line for the new videos. That day,

though, I just wanted to go home and try out the stick. I went behind the house, where nobody could see me, and walked up and down. Right away the stick started diving.

I was excited. It probably sounds dumb, but knowing that I could sense water under the ground changed things. It wouldn't make me rich and famous. I mean, you can't pick up the paper and see ads saying WATER WITCH WANTED. But I felt different—kind of special.

I remembered telling Marty, "Anything's possible." But I didn't really believe it then. Now I did—in a way.

When Dad came home, he'd already heard the story at the store. "My son, the witch," he said when he climbed out of his pickup.

"Come out in the back," I told him.

He laughed. "What are you going to do, zap me?"

"I want you to feel this."

He sighed and came over. "I'll bet it doesn't work for me."

"Good attitude, Dad."

I showed him how to hold the stick, and he walked about ten feet, then handed me the stick. "That's okay," he said. "One witch is enough for any family."

"Try it with me," I said.

He got a funny smile on his face. "You go ahead."

"Come on, Dad. I want you to see what it's like."

He sighed again and took hold of the stick. We walked around the yard, holding hands and waving the stick in front of us. "I hope none of the neighbors is watching," Dad said. "They'll think we've gone over the edge."

The point of the stick bobbed a little. I looked up at Dad. "You feel that?"

"I guess."

I took him to the spot where I'd felt the strongest pull. The stick bounced up and down. "You see what I mean?"

He laughed. "Well, the stick's moving."

"You think I'm doing it?"

He shrugged.

"I'm just holding the stick," I said.

Dad shook his head. "That's amazing," he said. But I wasn't sure he believed any of it.

I wasn't really surprised. Dad was always straight-up and sensible. And water witching wasn't sensible. It worked, but it didn't make any sense.

Three

On Saturday mornings Dad always put a jazz record on the stereo and cooked something fancy. I think it was his way to remember Mom. She'd always made a big deal out of Saturday morning, the one day when we weren't in a hurry.

There's no good way to tell this, so let me say it straight out: My mother was killed in a car accident two years ago. You don't get over something like that, but you sort of get used to it. A while back I saw a guy who'd had his hand cut off in a sawmill. He'd learned to get along with one hand and a stump, but of course it wasn't the same. That's the way Dad and I were without Mom. We just got along.

We usually didn't waste much time on cooking. For dinner we threw a steak or chops in the broiler, put potatoes in the microwave, and whipped up a green salad. Breakfast was cereal and fruit. But on Saturdays, Dad would make corn muffins or French toast or blueberry waffles.

That Saturday we had pancakes with fresh strawberries on

top. Dad hummed along with the music and looked out the window. While I ate, I kept thinking about holding that stick and feeling the surge through my arms. I don't think either of us said a word the whole meal.

After breakfast, I cleaned up the dishes while Dad threw our woodcutting gear into the pickup. Uncle Gene had asked Dad to cut up a big oak that had fallen across the road onto his place. The county road crew was supposed to take care of things like that, but it might be Halloween before they got around to it.

We didn't need the wood. We still had enough stacked up beside the house to keep our stove going for another winter. But Dad was too softhearted to say no.

The road to Uncle Gene's was actually about ten roads, and I might have gotten lost on my own. The mountains behind Alder Creek were crisscrossed with old roads put in years ago for logging or mining. You'd be driving along, and every little while you'd come to an unmarked fork, with both roads looking the same—two ruts through the brush. And a quarter mile down each road would be another fork.

Dad was in no danger of getting lost. He worked for the Forest Service, planning and supervising tree planting projects. He knew that back country and those old roads better than anybody, even Uncle Gene and Dr. Vincent.

It took us a couple of hours to clear the road and cut up the tree. Uncle Gene showed up in his Jeep and tried to help. He could have helped more by staying out of the way.

I filled the Jeep with wood and loaded our pickup until the fenders almost touched the tires. Half the wood was still lying on the ground. "I don't want to make another trip out here for that little bit," Dad told Uncle Gene. "You mind hauling off the rest?"

"I'll take care of it," Uncle Gene said.

Dad climbed into the pickup. "Well, thanks for letting me in on this. We needed some good oak."

Uncle Gene waved us off. "You're sure welcome."

That was Dad's way. He'd left Uncle Gene enough wood to last all next winter and ended up saying thank you.

We crawled along about five miles an hour, hoping the springs and tires would hold. A couple miles from town, we came up behind a brown Chevy pickup that was pulled off in the ditch with its hood up. A man in a baseball cap was sitting on the back bumper.

I recognized the ratty truck right away from its red camper shell and black rear fender. I'd seen it parked in front of the old Hartman place the week before. I was curious what kind of guy would move into a rundown house like that. The little kids called it the spook house.

Dad stopped the pickup and rolled down the window. "Need some help?"

The man walked back toward us. Up close, he looked older. His face was brown with big wrinkles, like he'd been looking into the sun all his life. "Great place to have engine trouble, right?" He laughed and took a can of snuff from his pocket. He held out the can, and Dad waved it away. "Yes, sir. I can really pick my places." He opened the can, took a fat pinch, and shoved it into his cheek. "Little tiny hole in the radiator hose. Didn't even know it till the engine got hot. Looked like somebody had stuck a needle in there. Little tiny spray of water."

"I have some friction tape in the toolbox," Dad said.

"So did we," the man said. "We got the hose fixed in about half a minute. But the radiator was dry by then. Me and my brother-in-law, we flipped a coin, and he lost. So he took the bucket and went down in the canyon for some water."

I leaned back in the seat, thinking about asking Marty to spend the night. Maybe we could rent a couple of the new videos.

"You can ride back to Alder Creek with us," Dad said.

"That's okay," the man said. "My brother-in-law'll be back any minute. He'd be real upset if he hauled water all the way up here and then we didn't need it."

Just then I felt a surge through my wrists and up to my elbows. It felt like I had that forked stick in my hands again. But this time the stick wasn't being pulled down toward the ground. It was being pushed back.

You know how magnets work against each other when you put the wrong sides together? I was getting that kind of feeling.

The man was lying. I was sure of it. He had a big grin on his wrinkled face, and his voice was slow and easy. But the surge kept running through my arms, pushing them back.

"Amos Lawlor's my name," the man said. He reached into the pickup to shake Dad's hand.

"Ken Thompson," Dad said. "And this is Sam."

Lawlor waved to me. "You from around here?"

"Alder Creek," Dad said.

"I just moved up here," Lawlor said. "Nice country." He turned his head and spit. "You can slide your rig on by. There's plenty of room. We'll be along directly."

"I can wait around if you want," Dad said.

Lawlor shook his head. "No, go ahead. He'll be back any minute. When he finds out he didn't have to do all that work, he'll have a cow." He laughed and stepped back. "Serves him right. It was his idea to drive up here. He came to visit us, and right away he wanted to go look at some land for sale. But, of course, he couldn't take his car."

The current kept running through my arms.

Dad put the truck in gear. "If you're sure."

Lawlor waved us on. "Go ahead."

It was a tight squeeze, but we made it past. The radiator cap was sitting on the fender, and I saw black tape wrapped around a hose. But those things didn't change my mind at all.

"Dad," I said, once we were beyond the pickup, "that guy was lying."

Dad looked over at me. "About what?"

"I don't know." I realized how stupid that sounded. "But he was lying. I could feel it—just the way I could feel water yesterday."

"Maybe so," Dad said, smiling and shaking his head. I could tell he didn't believe a word of it.

I didn't say any more. How could I explain something I didn't understand myself? I had no idea where the surges came from or why I was suddenly getting them. I just knew that Lawlor was lying.

I had to hurry back up there and find out what Lawlor was really doing. That way, I'd have proof that I was right. But I was already sure—without any proof at all.

When we got home, Dad backed the pickup next to the

empty spot where we'd put the new wood. "Dad," I said, "can I stack the wood later? I have something I want to do first."

"Okay," he said, "but I want it off the truck this afternoon."

I ran for the shed and got my bicycle. I hopped on it and headed back up the road.

My bike was the only really expensive thing I owned. It had eighteen gears and fat knobby tires and special wide fenders to protect me from flying mud. Not exactly a speed-burner, but the perfect bike for the dirt roads around Alder Creek. With the bike in the lowest gears, I could climb just about any hill a pickup could.

I zipped past the store, waving to Mrs. Lopez, and headed on up the road. I'd gone about half a mile when I heard a whistle behind me. I glanced back and saw Carmen pedaling toward me. I coasted to a stop and waited for her.

Except for a special padded seat, her bike was exactly like mine. Both of them had come from the same bike shop in Yreka. She always rode with her head about six inches above the handlebars. It looked uncomfortable to me, but that was her way. And nobody was going to change her.

She skidded to a stop beside me. "Where you going, Sam?"

"Dad and I saw a guy on the back roads. I think he's up to something. I want to take another look."

"I'll go along." Carmen isn't the kind to wait for an invitation.

She's a year younger than I am, but about my height. Maybe even an inch taller. Dad always says she's a beauty, but that seems like the wrong word. Not that Carmen is ugly or anything. But "beauty" makes me think of long-haired girls who wear lipstick and dresses. Carmen wears jeans and sweatshirts, and her brown hair isn't much longer than mine.

"We won't do anything," I said. "We'll just look."

"Let's go then." She shoved off and started to pedal.

We rode along side by side. As usual, we ended up in a kind of race, each of us trying to get just a little ahead. We were both breathing hard when we rounded a curve and saw the brown pickup, the hood still up. I hit my brakes.

We turned our bikes around and coasted back out of sight. Then we hauled our bikes over the bank and put them behind a stand of pine trees. "Why don't you wait here?" I said. "I'll be back in a minute."

Carmen gave me a disgusted look. "Fat chance."

We crossed the road and headed uphill. We planned to scoot through the brush and slip in close to the pickup. The idea was all right, but it was tough to work our way through the thickets of scrub oak without making any noise.

We crawled the last hundred feet or so and ended up at the edge of the road, about twenty feet behind the pickup. We lay in the leaves under some buckbrush and looked around. Nothing was moving.

Carmen moved close and whispered, "Now what do we do?"

"We wait."

Carmen rolled her eyes but didn't say anything.

I lay there and stared at that red camper shell. The back of the shell was a door that would swing up. At the bottom of that door was a silver handle, the kind you give a quarter of a turn and lift.

I kept twisting my wrist, making that quarter of a turn. "I can't stand it any longer," I whispered. "I'll be right back."

I slid out from under the bush and crept onto the road. I looked in both directions, then raced to the pickup. I gave that handle a twist and felt the mechanism slide.

The shell door popped open, and I raised it and stuck my head inside. Stretched out on the bed of the pickup was a dead deer, a bullet hole in its neck. I felt sick and disgusted. Deer season was five months off, and the doe in front of me wouldn't have been legal even then.

"Don't you move, boy!" The voice drilled into me like an electric shock.

Lawlor came charging up the bank and onto the road. I was too surprised to run.

"What are you doin'?" he shouted.

I couldn't think of a thing to say. I stepped away from the pickup and stood there with my mouth open.

"What's the matter with you?" he shouted. He grabbed the front of my shirt and pushed me back against the truck. "Don't play stupid with me. I want to know what you're up to."

I just stared at him.

"Sammy Joe, you get back here!" It was Carmen. She was standing beside the road.

Lawlor let go of my shirt and spun in her direction.

"Sammy Joe, you're gonna catch it," she screeched. "Daddy's gonna whip you good!"

"What's going on?" Lawlor asked her.

"That Sammy Joe," Carmen said. "He's doin' it again. He'll

climb into people's cars, hop on the backs of trucks. Just wants to go places. Last month he got all the way to Medford, and then he didn't have no idea how to get home."

If those lies of Carmen's sent surges up my arms, I was shaking too much to notice.

She pointed her finger at me. "You get back to the house right this minute. Daddy's gonna fix your wagon."

When she said that, I finally realized that Lawlor had his back to me. I raced around the pickup and ran down the road. When I was almost to the curve, I took one glance back and saw that nobody was following.

Once I was out of sight of the pickup, I crawled into the brush and waited. In just a minute I heard Carmen come crashing toward me. When she saw me, we headed uphill and stopped behind a stand of black oaks.

"Thanks, Carmen," I said. "You were amazing."

She smiled. "I don't know if he believed me or not. He was just so surprised, he couldn't figure it all out. When you took off running, I just said, 'Sorry, mister,' and headed into the brush."

"I owe you one," I said.

"Did you see anything in there?"

"A deer," I said. "The guy's a poacher. He probably has another one down in the canyon."

"That slime," Carmen muttered. "We'll fix him."

I leaned against a tree, trying to sort things out. For a minute I wanted to tell her about the surges. But it was too crazy. She probably would have laughed.

Ten minutes later we heard the pickup go tearing past. We

hurried to our bicycles and rode back to the Alder Creek Store. I used the pay phone there to call Fish and Game. The guy who took my information must have been the world's slowest writer.

Afterward, Carmen and I sat on the porch of the store and had a Coke. "You know," she said, "I like the name Sammy Joe for you. It kind of fits."

"Thanks a lot," I told her. "Sammy Joe, the dimwit. Just what I want to be."

"You know what?" she said. "I think we ought to get our story straight. If my mom hears what really happened, I'll be in deep trouble."

"Me too." I thought for a minute. "What if we were just riding along and we saw the guy shoving a deer into his pickup? That's simple enough, isn't it?"

"Simple and sneaky," she said. "I like it."

After finishing our Cokes, we wandered over to the bicycles. I had to go stack the wood, but I hated to leave. "Listen," I said, "are you doing anything tonight?"

Carmen looked at me, then looked away. "Yeah," she said, "I think we're having company."

I felt the surge in my arms again. The stick was being pushed away. I looked straight at Carmen. She was looking down at her bike, a half-smile on her face.

But she'd lied to me.

To me, things had seemed special. Too special for me just to go home and watch a video or something. I wanted to sit on Carmen's porch and talk about what we'd done. Maybe go for a walk.

But she had other ideas.

"See you later," I mumbled. I shoved off and headed my bicycle toward home.

"Bye, Sammy Joe," she called, sounding just as happy as ever.

It made you wonder about people.

Four

The telephone rang while Dad and I were eating dinner. Dad answered it, then waved me over. "It's Deputy Bates. He says he wants to talk to his assistant."

Deputy Bates was the officer assigned to our part of the county. I saw him at the store now and then—a tall, thin guy who was never in a hurry.

"Fish and Game called me about Lawlor," he said. "They didn't have a warden out this way, so I took care of it."

"Did you get him?"

"Guess what, Sam. The guy's innocent."

"Really?"

Bates laughed. "That's what he says. Two does hanging in his shed, and none of it's his fault. He claims the deer were hit by a car. He just took the carcasses home to feed to his dog."

"What did you do?" I asked.

"Laughed in his face and wrote out a citation. It's a rotten business, Sam. Some of these restaurants pay big money for deer meat, and sleazebags like him are cashing in."

"I'm glad you caught him," I said.

"Good job, Sam," Bates said. "I wrote you up for this. Maybe Fish and Game'll give you a little reward."

After the call, I had to tell Dad something. I thought about spilling the whole thing, then settled for a simple version: I'd gone up there to make sure Lawlor could get his pickup started, and I'd seen him put a deer in his truck.

Dad gave me a long look—long enough to make me wonder if he was getting surges. But he didn't ask any questions.

Next morning I rode my bike back up to where Lawlor's pickup had been parked. I was having trouble getting things straight, and I thought it might help to go back to the spot where I'd gotten the first surges. But it didn't.

Why had the surges suddenly started? I wondered if I'd had them before and just not known what they were. Maybe the water witching somehow helped me recognize them. But even if I could tell when people were lying, what good was that? If I'd been James Bond or some master spy, it would have been a great secret weapon. But how could I use it in Alder Creek?

Riding back to town, I wondered if I still had the power. I stopped at the store, bought a cup of hot chocolate, and carried it out on the porch where Mr. Lopez and Dr. Vincent were sitting. I sat on one of the side benches and waited.

Nothing happened for a long time. Dr. Vincent was talking about how much things would change in Alder Creek if we ever got the road paved. SOT and MOTSOT—I'd heard that almost as often as the litter lecture.

I stirred my chocolate and looked up toward the mountain. I wished somebody else would show up and give me a chance for a test.

Then Mr. Lopez said, "I'll tell you, I'm not sorry I moved here. I'd do it all over again."

The surges ran up my arm.

It was all I could do to keep from yelling out loud. I was amazed—both at the surges and at Mr. Lopez. He was always smiling and joking with the customers. Was he as bored as the rest of us?

Just then, Mrs. Lopez came out of the store. "Tony," she said, "would you move those crates into the storeroom? My back is sore." She looked over at Dr. Vincent. "I think I pulled something."

The surges shot up my arms. So Mrs. Lopez didn't have a sore back. She just didn't feel like hauling the crates.

Then she and Dr. Vincent talked about the weather. I wished I could figure some way to make them change the subject. When I heard a car coming, I settled back on my bench and hoped for a liar.

I got more than I hoped for. The brown pickup skidded to a stop by the gas pump, and Amos Lawlor climbed out. I started to move, but he spotted me right away. For just a second his cold eyes were fixed on mine. Then he turned away and smiled. I slid off the porch and headed up the alley. As soon as I was out of sight, I stopped and knelt down like I was tying my shoes.

"Dr. Vincent," Lawlor called out, "I was hoping I'd find you today."

"Good morning, Mr. Lawlor," Dr. Vincent said. "Can I buy you a cup of coffee?"

"Call me Amos." Lawlor's boots banged across the porch. "Listen, you know a deputy sheriff named Bates?"

"I know him," Dr. Vincent said.

"That guy's got it in for me," Lawlor said. "Making me look real bad. What happened, see, is yesterday I saw these two dead deer lying by the road. Somebody'd hit 'em and left 'em. I always feel bad when I see an animal killed that way. You know what I mean?"

The surges ran through me so hard that I couldn't keep my hands still.

"I hate to see things wasted," Lawlor was saying. "I figured I'd take those deer home and feed 'em to my dogs. I couldn't see no harm in that."

He went on and on. Dr. Vincent and Mrs. Lopez ate up every word, telling Lawlor it wasn't fair. Dr. Vincent said he knew a good lawyer.

"I don't mind paying the fine," Lawlor said. "But my wife and I just moved in here. We'd hate for people to think bad of us." He sounded so sad and serious, I would have believed him too—if the surges hadn't been shooting past my elbows.

When I'd had all I could stand, I went up the alley and sat down by the storeroom. From there, I couldn't hear what anybody was saying. That suited me fine.

That afternoon I stopped at the store for some root beer, then rode my bike over to Marty's place. I had to talk to somebody, and Marty was my only choice. He lived about three miles from me—two miles down the county road and a mile back up a canyon. The McNabbs had bought a log cabin on some acreage that bordered on Forest Service land. They didn't have any close neighbors, and that's the way they liked it. They'd moved to Alder Creek to get away from crowds.

Like a lot of people in the back country, they had no telephone or electricity. Most people like them had portable generators for lights, but Mrs. McNabb hated the noise of a generator. So they used kerosene lanterns. They weren't complete pioneers though. They used bottled gas for cooking and for the refrigerator, and they listened to music on a battery-powered tape player. But they didn't have a VCR.

The McNabbs had a chicken-wire fence around their property, with three strands of barbed wire at the top and NO TRESPASSING signs every twenty feet. The padlocked metal gate looked like the entrance to a prison. I got the key from its hiding place under a flat rock and opened the gate far enough to haul my bike through. I always felt like a burglar going in there.

In the mile from the gate to their cabin, the driveway forded the creek three times. On a bicycle you could make the ride and stay dry, but it was tricky. You had to build up your speed, then lift your feet high just as your front tire hit the water.

By the time I made my third crossing, the guinea hens were already squawking. They were the watchdogs of the place. Their squawking got the ducks and turkeys going.

As usual, Mrs. McNabb had her easel set up between the rows of plants that surrounded the cabin. She did watercolors, mostly outdoor scenes. She'd paint for a while, then pull weeds, then paint some more. "Hello, Samuel," she called. Turkey chicks skittered around by her feet.

I waved, saw that she had a brush in her hand, and rode on past. When she was gardening, she liked company, but when she was painting, she was off limits.

I found Marty in the little shed behind their cabin. He was loading greenware into the pottery kiln. "There he is," he called out. "The witch of Alder Creek." He closed the door of the kiln and fussed with the dials. All three of the McNabbs made pottery when they got in the mood—heavy mugs and bowls with a blue-green glaze. Marty said they could sell all the pottery they made, but they only earned three or four dollars an hour. Not exactly big money, but it paid for groceries when nothing else was selling.

"So, Mr. Witch, what's new and exciting down in Alder Creek? SOT and MOTSOT?"

For once, I had an answer to that: "NOTSOT."

I told him about Amos Lawlor and the possible reward, but I stayed with the story Carmen and I had decided to use. I was dying to talk about the other stuff, but the time didn't seem right.

After Marty cleaned up the pottery shed, we went over to the barn. Mr. McNabb was up on a ladder, welding a chain to the top of a huge metal statue that could have been an elephant or a dinosaur. "What's he making?" I whispered to Marty.

"Something big," Marty said.

Marty pointed at the brush buggy, and his dad nodded. The buggy was made from a wrecked Volkswagen. His dad had taken off the car body and shortened the frame. What was left was two seats right down on the axle, four tires, and an engine in back. The buggy only had two gears—forward and reverse—and the top speed was around ten miles an hour, but it would go almost anywhere. Marty couldn't drive it on the county road, of course, but the mountains behind his place were crisscrossed with fire trails and old logging roads.

Trout season opened in six days, so we checked out some of our old fishing spots. Then we drove farther out, following the ridge trail. Marty stopped at the top of a rise. From there, we could see Mt. Shasta, a good sixty miles away. Marty shut off the engine and got our root beer out of the little cooler strapped behind the driver's seat.

Sitting there in the grass, listening to the clicks of the cooling motor, I told Marty the real story about Lawlor. He kept watching my face while I talked.

"You're serious, aren't you?" he asked finally.

"Yeah."

"You're a human lie detector, huh?" He scooted around so that he was sitting right in front of me. "Okay, let's test it out." He put his root beer can behind him and kept both hands back there.

"Give me a break," I said.

"Let's try it. I have the can in my left hand. True or false? Am I lying or not?"

I took a drink from my can and leaned back. "I don't know."

"Come on. Am I lying or not?"

I looked at him. I didn't get any feeling at all. "I guess not."

Marty grinned. "It's in my right hand now. Am I lying or not?"

I shrugged. "I can't tell. I don't think so."

"Now it's in my left again. True or not? Come on. Tell me."

"Cut it out," I said. "I don't have the feeling at all."

"You sure don't," he said. "The can was on the ground the whole time. So it was all lies." He laughed and took a drink.

"I'm just telling you what happened," I said. "I don't care if you believe it or not."

"I believe it." Marty wasn't laughing anymore. "You said it, and I believe it." He reached over with his foot and kicked my shoe. "Come on. You had a feeling about something, and it was right. What's the problem?"

I let it go.

Afterward, I got Marty to drive over to Uncle Gene's. I was hoping to get some answers from the old guy, which was a stupid idea. How was I going to get answers when I hadn't even figured out the questions?

There were two ways to get from Alder Creek to Uncle Gene's, both of them slow and rough. One way was to take a pickup over the snaky roads that Dad and I had taken the day before. The other was to walk or take our brush buggy along the fire trails that followed the ridge line. With the brush buggy, we still had to do the last quarter mile on foot, working our way downhill through the manzanita and scrub oak to Uncle Gene's clearing at the bottom of the canyon.

It was ten miles by the road or four miles cross country. Most of the time Uncle Gene walked to Alder Creek. It wasn't as fast that way, but his legs were more dependable than his old Jeep.

While Marty and I hiked into the canyon, we hollered for

Uncle Gene until he answered us with his coyote howl. He was always worried about somebody coming to steal his maps. And he kept a shotgun close by, just in case.

Uncle Gene was sitting on the steps of his cabin with a stack of old papers beside him. Leonard was grazing beside the cabin along with the two sheep. Uncle Gene had bought those sheep after somebody told him that Leonard would be happier if he had company. Maybe he was. He herded those sheep all over the place. But he still spit.

Marty and I came past the corral and walked toward the cabin with our faces turned away from Leonard. He usually didn't spit unless you looked at him. Uncle Gene took off his thick reading glasses and set them on top of the papers. "You two out looking for trouble again?" he called out.

"You bet," I said.

"Hi, Uncle Gene," Marty called out.

Marty and I headed straight for the faucet by the steps. It was only a foot tall, so we had to get on our knees to drink. "You boys don't have to bend over that way," Uncle Gene said. "I can get you a glass."

"That's all right," I said. I'd seen his glasses. They looked like Leonard had drunk out of them.

Uncle Gene opened the door of the cabin and set the papers inside. "Been checking things over," he said. "Soon as I get that hundred dollars, I'll get my grubstake and head out."

"I thought you were getting your money yesterday," I said. "Didn't Deputy Bates come?"

"He came all right, him and some government men. No argument this time. The whole setup was plain as day. I didn't need my pictures at all. But don't tell nobody, hear? Next day or two, they're gonna fly over the area in an airplane, see if they can spot the guy that planted the stuff."

"Why didn't you get the money?" I asked him.

"I'll get it," Uncle Gene said. "Sheriff'll send it to me this week."

"Maybe," Marty muttered.

"He will if he knows what's good for him." Then Uncle Gene smiled at me. "You ready to do a little more witching?"

"Not really," I said.

He laughed. "Surprised you, didn't it? I wish I'd had my camera out. You shoulda seen the look on your face."

I didn't care about finding water anymore, but Uncle Gene wouldn't listen. He reached under the steps and got out a forked stick. Then he took us up the hill toward the old mine shaft. "There's an underground spring up here," he said. "Let's see if you can find it." Leonard and the sheep followed along behind us.

Uncle Gene had me guess how far underground the water was. Whenever I guessed, he'd laugh, but he wouldn't say if I was right or not. The whole thing got old in a hurry. Marty wandered away and lay down in the entrance to the mine shaft. "It's cooler in here," he said.

In the early days some miner had tunneled back about fifty feet into the mountain, following a vein of gold. In the winter, when it was too rainy to work outside, Uncle Gene sometimes dug around in there, getting a little color.

With Marty out of the way, I asked the question I'd come to ask: "Uncle Gene, did you ever get those feelings when you didn't have the stick in your hands? Did you ever just feel the pull?"

He gave me a funny look, then laughed. "If I told you everything, you wouldn't believe me. You'd figure I was just a crazy old man flapping his jaws."

"No, I wouldn't," I said. "Listen, yesterday a guy was talking, and I got those same feelings, except they were pushing me away. So I knew he was lying."

Uncle Gene looked over at Leonard. "Some things you don't want to talk about too much," he said.

And that was all he'd say. And I didn't even know if he meant me or him. It wasn't worth climbing down into the canyon for that. And it sure wasn't worth the climb back out.

Marty thought the whole thing was funny. On our way uphill he kept after me: "Hey, witch, I got a feeling in my stomach. Does that mean there's water around here, or does it mean somebody's lying, or does it mean I'm about to burp?"

"None of those," I said. "It means you're turning into a dork."

Five

Riding my bicycle home from Marty's, I decided to forget the whole thing. What good was a lie detector that only worked part of the time? And who wanted to be a lie detector anyway? I stopped by the store, rented a video that was all car crashes and gun battles, and watched it twice.

When I returned the video the next morning, Mrs. Lopez was behind the counter. "You hear about Mr. Harrison?" she asked.

I shook my head.

"He was over in Yreka yesterday. Stepped off a curb and broke his ankle. He's in the hospital."

"Is Mrs. McNabb going to be our teacher?" Marty's mother was our usual substitute.

"Not this time," Mrs. Lopez said. "Dr. Vincent said there's a woman who just moved here. She has a regular teaching credential."

I tried not to smile. I felt sorry for Mr. Harrison, but I was glad for any kind of change. "How long will Mr. Harrison be out?"

Mrs. Lopez shrugged. "Who knows? Maybe a week or two. Not too long, I hope. He's a good teacher."

I got a tiny surge up my arm. Or maybe I just thought I did.

The school was locked when I got there. Carmen and I sat on the steps and watched the little ones play tag. I told her about Deputy Bates's phone call and the possible reward. "So what'll we buy with it?" I asked her.

She looked at me and laughed. "I get some of this big money?"

"You bet. Fifty-fifty split."

"That's nice," she said. "But I wouldn't spend it yet."

"You don't think we'll get it?"

She shook her head. "You know how those rewards go."

"Then I've got a deal for you. If we get any money, we'll throw a big graduation party. How's that?"

"That's not fair," she said. "I'm not graduating."

"What difference does it make?" I said. "You don't think we'll get any money anyway."

"All right. I'll be generous. We'll throw a graduation party." She held up a finger. "Except . . ."

"Except what?"

"If the reward's more than twenty dollars, we have another vote."

That was typical Carmen.

When the schoolbus pulled in, Dr. Vincent was behind the wheel. Everybody crowded around him. The little kids were disappointed that he wasn't wearing his shorts.

"Are you going to be our teacher?" somebody asked.

"Just for an hour or so," he said.

Everybody went "Aww," except Bobby Keck. He asked, "Do you have your shorts on under your pants?"

"Be glad you don't have to ride the bus," Marty told me. "Dr. Vincent's a horrible driver. He was talking away about pine cones and ran a truck off the road."

"He's worse than Mr. Harrison?" I asked.

"He's worse than anybody," Marty said. "If he's driving this afternoon, I'll walk home. I don't want to end up in the hospital with Mr. Harrison."

First Dr. Vincent had us make get well cards. Then we had a boring lecture about flowers that got the little kids squirming. Then silent reading. Dr. Vincent ended up standing by the windows, where he could see the road.

"Here she comes," he announced.

We all stood up and looked. A brown pickup stopped in front of the school. I stared at the red camper shell and the black fender. It had to be a mistake.

A big woman climbed out of the pickup and headed for the school. She had gray hair tied in a bun and a green tent dress. She would have looked fine—like somebody's grandmother—if she hadn't gotten out of that pickup.

"Can you believe it?" Carmen whispered to me.

"Take your seats, boys and girls," Dr. Vincent said, pushing open the door.

"Good morning, Dr. Vincent," the woman said. "I came as soon as I could."

"Boys and girls," Dr. Vincent announced, "let me introduce your new teacher, Mrs. Lawlor."

Dr. Vincent left right away. Then Mrs. Lawlor stood by the

blackboard and looked us over. "Let's make everything perfectly clear," she said. "I know how substitute teachers get treated in some places. That's not going to happen here. You will stay in your seats, and you will not make a sound. Are there any questions?"

"Welcome to the Twilight Zone," Marty muttered.

Things stayed pretty quiet that morning. The little kids had a tough time though. They kept raising their hands, the way they always did. Mrs. Lawlor came around and tried to help, but pretty soon she was saying things like, "Can't you figure out anything for yourself?" and "Skip it if you don't know how to do it."

Just after eleven o'clock, Mrs. Lawlor tapped on her desk. "I have to take my medicine," she said. "I'll be right outside, so I'd better not hear any noise."

The minute the door closed, of course, people were making faces and holding their noses. Bobby Keck crept back and peeked out the door. "She's not there," he whispered.

We looked out the windows, but she wasn't there either. That meant she was on the other side of the building, away from the road. The only windows on that side are up high, too high for anybody to see out.

Unless they're sneaky—which we were.

One of the girls watched the door while Marty stood on a desk. Then I lifted Bobby Keck up to him. Marty boosted Bobby up to the window.

"She's smokin' a cigarette," Bobby said, loud enough to send all of us scrambling for our seats. The idea of a teacher sneaking out for a smoke struck me funny, and I liked her a little better after that.

On Monday afternoons, we had Circle Time. We put our desks in a circle and talked. Sometimes people told what they'd done over the weekend, if anybody had done anything. And sometimes we told stories, with each person adding a sentence to the story.

Mrs. Lawlor said we could have Circle Time, but we had to write down five things about ourselves. That way, she could get to know us. "I can't write that good," Bobby Keck told her. She said he could draw pictures of his five things.

When some kids couldn't think of five things, Mrs. Lawlor said they could write down stuff they liked to eat. So that's what most people did.

I wondered what she'd say if I wrote, "I'm a witch." Or "I caught your husband poaching deer." I even thought about writing that my mother was dead. Instead, I wrote about videos I liked and fishing and my bike.

We moved the desks into a circle, and everybody read the answers. Half the little kids said they liked peanut butter. When we got to Mrs. Lawlor, she asked, "Am I supposed to talk too?"

"Sure," Marty told her. Mr. Harrison never talked during Circle Time, but after Marty said that, we all nodded.

"Well," she said, looking around the circle, "I've just moved here. The house where I live needs a lot of work. That's what I'll use my teacher's pay for. I grew up in Bend, Oregon. I'm a graduate of Oregon State University."

A surge rushed through my fingers and up toward my elbows. The muscles in my forearms went tight. I grabbed the sides of my desk to keep my hands down. I kept my eyes on the floor and tried to think of something else, but it didn't help. I knew she was lying.

Marty poked me in the side with his finger. "You all right?" he whispered.

I nodded but kept my eyes on the floor.

By then, Aurelia Lopez was talking. I leaned back in my seat and watched Mrs. Lawlor out of the corner of my eye. She was sitting straight in her chair, smiling and nodding. A little of her hair had pulled out of the bun and was hanging over her ear. She didn't look like a liar. But I knew she was.

At recess, I got Marty off to the side. "Do me a favor, all right?"

Marty looked at me. "Is this a joke?"

"I'm serious," I said. "When we go back inside, ask Mrs. Lawlor about Oregon State."

"Ask her what?"

"Anything," I said. "Tell her you're thinking about going there. Ask her if it's a good school. Anything."

"What's going on?" Marty asked. "Are you starting that lie detector stuff again?"

"Just do it," I said. "I'll explain later."

When Mrs. Lawlor called us inside, Marty stopped beside her. "I was thinking about going to Oregon State," he said. "Did you have fun there?"

"You don't go to college to have fun," she said.

"Was it hard?"

"Some classes were," Mrs. Lawlor said. "But that's good. I learned a lot in those hard classes."

The surges ran up my arms again. She was lying.

As soon as we sat down, Marty leaned toward me and asked, "So what's the deal?"

"She's lying," I told him.

"About what?"

"I don't know."

Marty shook his head. "That's a big help."

The last hour of the day was terrible. By then, Billy Cavalo couldn't sit still any longer. When Billy got antsy that way, Mr. Harrison would have him run around the schoolhouse ten times. Or sometimes Billy just went outside and played trucks in the sandpile.

Carmen tried to tell Mrs. Lawlor that, but Mrs. Lawlor said, "I've seen show-offs before." Every time Billy got out of his seat, which was every minute or two, she grabbed him by the ear and hauled him back. "You sit there and don't move," she told him.

Billy would nod, and the tears would run down his cheeks. And two minutes later he'd be crawling in the aisle.

The only break we got was when Mrs. Lawlor went outside for another smoke.

When school was finally over, Marty's father showed up to drive the bus. "Dr. Vincent's no dummy," Marty said. "He's too smart to ride in a bus he's driving."

After the bus left, I went up to Mrs. Lawlor. I wanted to make sure I was right. "Could I ask you something?" I said.

She smiled at me. "Of course."

That made me feel crummy, but I went ahead. "How long do you have to go to school to be a teacher?"

"It all depends," she said.

"Do you just have to graduate from college, or do you have to take extra courses after that?"

Her mouth was still smiling, but her eyes weren't. "The rules are different in different states."

"I'm thinking about being a teacher," I told her. If she'd had my powers, that lie would have sent shock waves through her. "Did you take extra courses after you graduated?"

"Yes," she said. "Lots of them."

I felt the surge again. There was no doubt at all.

At dinner I told Dad, "There's something wrong with Mrs. Lawlor."

"Probably is," Dad said. "Otherwise she wouldn't be married to a poacher."

"Besides that," I said. "I don't think she's really a teacher. She's lying about where she went to school."

Dad looked at me. "How do you know?"

"I just do." There was no point in saying any more.

"That's not good enough, Sam," he said. "You can't go around saying things like that without any proof."

"I'm not going around saying things," I said. "I'm just telling you. And how am I supposed to get proof?"

"You're right. Erase that last statement." He waved his hand in the air, erasing an imaginary blackboard.

"There's something wrong about her," I said. "She isn't what she says she is. And she's mean to Billy Cavalo besides."

Dad pushed away his plate. "How sure are you?"

"Positive," I said.

He sat for a minute, then went into the other room and telephoned Dr. Vincent. "Someone raised the question," I heard him say. "I think we need to check her papers very carefully."

It was a long conversation. Every little while Dad would say, "I understand that, but I still think we should check."

The next day seemed to last a month. Mrs. Lawlor had us work silently at our desks all day. And Billy Cavalo ended up standing in the corner—except that he kept wandering away and getting dragged back there. The only good thing was that Mrs. Lawlor took plenty of medicine breaks.

When Dad came home from work, he asked, "How was school?"

"Terrible," I said. "I think Mr. Harrison planned it all. This way, everybody will love him when he gets back."

Dad bent over and unlaced his boots. "Want some good news?"

"I could use some," I said.

"Tomorrow you get Mrs. McNabb."

"Great," I said. "What happened?"

Dad smiled. "Dr. Vincent says there may be some questions about Mrs. Lawlor's background."

"So he fired her?"

Dad pulled off his boots and set them by the door. "Not exactly. I don't know how much proof he had. And he didn't want any bad feelings. So he told her some parents complained about her smoking. Which was true, I guess."

"Just so she's out of there," I said.

Dad stood and looked at me for a minute. "How'd you know she wasn't a real teacher?"

I wanted to tell him the truth, but I knew he wouldn't

believe it. "Listen," I said, "if you watched her trying to teach, you'd know it too."

The next morning while I was walking to school, I saw Lawlor's pickup coming. I hunched down and turned my head away. The pickup skidded to a stop right beside me. Lawlor leaned out the window and said, "Think you're real smart, don't you? Went and squealed on me."

I kept walking with my eyes straight ahead. Lawlor shifted the pickup into reverse and backed up so that he stayed even with me.

"What about my wife? You squeal on her too?" He spit in my direction. "What kind of place is this? All the kids a bunch of little sissy tattletales?"

I went on walking, wishing somebody would come along. He kept backing up, staying right with me. "You better watch yourself," he said. "You start making trouble, and you'll end up in the middle of it every time."

"Leave me alone."

"You stay outa my way," Lawlor said. "I don't even want to see you. You ever butt into my business again, you're gonna be real sorry." He spit again, then shifted gears and drove off.

Six

You're getting really spooky," Marty told me. "You could read Mrs. Lawlor's mind, couldn't you?"

"It's not like that," I said.

Marty shrugged. "Whatever it is, it's weird."

"Just don't tell anybody, all right?"

He looked away.

"Who'd you tell?" I asked.

His head snapped up. "Now you're doing it to *me*."

"There's nothing magic about it. I know that look on your face. Who'd you tell?"

"Just my mother. She's into some of that stuff. I tried to ask about it, and right away she thought I was talking about myself. So I told her the whole thing. I'm sorry."

"It doesn't matter," I said.

But it did matter. That first morning Mrs. McNabb brought me a bunch of books on ESP. "These might interest you," she said.

When she turned her back, I looked over at Marty.

"Thanks a lot, buddy. Any time I have a secret, I'll know who not to tell."

"I don't have to bother answering that," Marty said. "You can read my mind and see what names I'm calling you."

I held my hand over my eyes for a second. "No use," I said. "Your mind's a big blank page."

He laughed, and we let it go. When you only have one friend, you can't stay mad at him.

That afternoon, Uncle Gene showed up just when school was out. All the little kids had to pat his beard, so the bus got held up a few minutes.

After the bus left, Uncle Gene hauled a letter out of his pocket and showed it to Mrs. McNabb. "What do you think about this? It says I won a free trip to Reno."

Mrs. McNabb opened the envelope. Inside were some blue and yellow papers, along with a fifty-dollar bill. She read the letter, then folded it carefully. "Congratulations, Uncle Gene."

"What's wrong with it?" he asked.

"Nothing," Mrs. McNabb said. "You take the special bus Saturday morning from Yreka. You spend Saturday night in a nice hotel. They pay for all your meals, and you have fifty dollars for spending money."

Uncle Gene shook his head. "Sounds fishy to me."

"I don't see any catch," Mrs. McNabb said. "You better go and have a good time."

"I can't drive all the way to Yreka."

"You wouldn't have to," Mrs. McNabb said. "On Saturday morning you can get a ride with Carl Keck. He goes in early for the flea market. And I can pick you up Sunday afternoon. How's that?"

Uncle Gene took the letter from her. "Do I have to spend the money?"

Mrs. McNabb laughed. "You ought to. You ought to have some fun. But you don't have to spend a dime if you don't want to. You have vouchers for the bus ride and the hotel and your meals."

"Sounds fishy to me," Uncle Gene said again.

We found out later that he'd already had Mr. Lopez read the letter. And Dr. Vincent. And probably some others. Everybody told him the same thing, but he still wasn't sure.

"He's right," Mrs. McNabb told Marty and me after Uncle Gene had gone. "It is fishy. It's not a business thing. No business sends you fifty-dollar bills. Somebody's giving Uncle Gene a present."

All that week I kept getting little surges. Mr. Lopez was lying about his mother-in-law. Jenny Cavalo was lying about her horse doing tricks. Aurelia was lying about the book she was reading.

People lied about the dumbest things—how much they paid for their cars, how many hours of sleep they got, how much they ate. It was funny sometimes, but it made me wonder if there was such a thing as an honest person.

On Thursday Mrs. McNabb had me stay after school. "I thought you might want to talk about your gift," she said.

"Not really." She kept smiling at me, and I ended up

saying, "It's not that big a deal. Sometimes I can tell when people are lying, that's all."

"That could be scary."

"I guess." I knew she wanted me to go on, but I didn't feel like it.

She told me about different people with special powers. I only half listened. I knew she'd get back to me sooner or later.

When she did, she surprised me. "Samuel," she said, "when was the last time you and your father talked about your mother?"

That question made me feel creepy. It was like having somebody poking through my dresser drawers. "I don't know."

She shook her head. "The two of you—you're keeping it all inside, aren't you?" She looked at me. "Have you talked about her this month?"

"I don't remember." I looked toward the door. "Listen, Mrs. McNabb, I have a lot of chores to do."

She put her hands on my shoulders and looked into my eyes. "Samuel, I don't want to embarrass you. But you and your father need to talk. Even if it's painful. You can't keep it bottled up."

"Okay." I tried to move back, but she kept hold of my shoulders.

"Will you do me a favor, Samuel? Tonight I want you to say something to your father about your mother. Anything at all. But say something."

"Okay." She let go of me, and I headed for the door.

"You've received a wonderful gift, Samuel," she called after me. "Relax and enjoy it and learn from it."

But if I'd had my choice of gifts, I'd rather have had a trip to Reno and a fifty-dollar bill.

While I was walking home, Carmen rode up beside me on her bicycle. "What's going on?" she asked. "You staying after school and making points with the teacher?"

"Yeah, sure."

Carmen kept pedaling just fast enough to stay even with me. "What's really going on, Sam?"

"SOT and MOTSOT," I said.

"I'm serious. I know something's happening to you. I asked Marty about it, and he said I should ask you."

"It's no big thing," I said. "Things are a little weird, that's all."

Carmen shoved down on the bike pedal so that her bike shot ahead of me. Then she turned my way and stopped, blocking my path. "Don't give me that. I want to know what's happening."

I stood and looked at her. "You're in my way," I said finally.

She gave me half a smile. "That's right. And I'm going to stay in your way until you tell me."

"Did it ever occur to you that this might not be any of your business?"

Her smile got bigger. "Yeah. But I want to know anyway." Then she looked me straight in the eye. "Besides, I care about you. So anything that happens to you *is* my business."

Carmen had never said anything like that before. And she kept looking straight at me, like she was daring me. So I went ahead and told her the whole story. She walked along beside me, pushing her bike. "Wow," she said when I finished.

"Right."

She looked over at me. "So you can tell when anybody's lying?"

"It's not that simple," I said. "Sometimes I get feelings, and sometimes I don't. Marty had me try on him, and I couldn't do a thing."

"What about me?" Carmen asked. "Could you tell if I was lying?"

I remembered last Saturday when she'd said she was busy, but I said, "Probably not."

I must have said it wrong because she stopped cold. "You've already done it, haven't you?"

I kept on walking. "Forget the whole thing. I didn't want to talk about it in the first place."

She came jogging up beside me and shoved the bike in front of me again. "Oh, no, you don't."

"Come on, Carmen," I said.

"I want to know right now." She glared at me. "If you're zapping me with your truth rays, I want to know it."

I reached out and gave the bike a push. "Lighten up, Carmen. How could I test it? You'd never lie to me."

But she wasn't about to laugh it off. "Tell me."

"It only happened once," I said. "Just for a second."

"When?"

"Saturday. When I asked if you were doing anything and you said you were having company."

Without saying a word, Carmen jerked her bike out of my way, climbed on it, and rode off. When she'd gone about a hundred yards, she made a circle and came back toward me.

"I didn't want to tell you any of that," I called out when she came close. "But you wouldn't let it be."

She stopped beside me. Her face was red, and her eyes were full of tears. "I want you to know one thing," she said. "I *did* lie. We weren't having company. Mom and Dad had been fighting all day. I didn't want you to come over and hear it."

"You didn't have to explain," I said.

"Oh, sure," she said between closed teeth. She jammed her foot onto the pedal and rode off.

Later on, I thought about going over to her house and telling her I was sorry. But I wasn't sure what I was sorry for.

I knew Mrs. McNabb would ask me the next day, so I tried to think of a question to ask Dad. When I started thinking about Mom, though, all the terrible things came back—the funeral, Dad staring at the wall for hours, the rainy nights when I lay in bed and cried, that first Christmas.

I couldn't think of a question.

When Mrs. McNabb took me aside the next morning, I lied to her. I said we'd had a good talk.

So I was a liar too. Why should I be any different?

Seven

Saturday was the opening day of trout season. Right then, nothing in the world sounded better than fishing in some lonely lake with just Marty around.

Dad had to work Saturday morning, but he planned to fish later on. So we still made our usual bets for the biggest fish—one bet for length, one for weight. The bets were only for five cents each, but they were serious business.

I crawled out of bed at daylight and had a quick bowl of corn flakes. I felt cheated, missing our usual Saturday morning feed, but opening day was special. When I went out the front door, Dad yelled from his bedroom, "I don't care how early you go, I'll still beat you."

I rode my bike over to Marty's. I had to wear a backpack to carry all my fishing gear and our root beer. We had our usual arrangement: Marty brought the sandwiches and I brought the drinks. Mrs. McNabb refused to buy soda. She called it slow poison.

Riding past the store, I saw Carl Keck and Uncle Gene

climbing into Carl's truck. So Uncle Gene was going to have his Reno holiday. "Have a good time," I called to him. He gave me a quick wave. From the look on his face, you would have thought he was heading for a funeral.

Marty and I took the brush buggy three miles up the ridge trail and parked it under a tree. Then we gathered up our equipment and started the long downhill climb through the thick chemise brush. There was no trail to Ricketts Lake, which is why we had the place to ourselves.

That morning the long climb was worth it. The trout fought each other for a chance at our hooks.

Marty and I use fly tackle and small unbarbed hooks so that we can release the fish without hurting them. With those smooth hooks, though, the fish can slip off if you don't bring them in just right. We let plenty of fish slip off that day, but we still caught and released dozens.

"It's too easy," Marty said. "And I love every minute."

When I'm fishing, I only keep enough for dinner—two trout. But I hadn't had a meal of trout for six months. The thought of those fish dipped in corn meal and frying in a pan made me so hungry that I kept an extra one.

We had an early lunch, then fished some more. When we'd had enough, we stripped off our clothes and jumped into the freezing lake. Then, with our teeth chattering, we pulled on our clothes and started back up the mountain toward the brush buggy. It made for a crazy trip. We started out shivering and ended up with the sweat pouring off us. Somewhere, halfway to the ridgetop, we were comfortable—for thirty seconds or so.

We always left two cans of root beer in the ice chest of the buggy. Thinking about that cold root beer helped us drag ourselves the last half mile. But that day the fishing had been too good for us to be dragging. We ended up racing, with the winner supposed to get both root beers.

When we came crashing out of the brush, I noticed that the buggy was sitting crooked. Marty let out a groan and stopped running. "Oh, man, a flat tire."

I groaned too. We didn't have a flat tire. We had *two* flat tires. Both tires on the driver's side had that squashed-out shape that tells you every bit of air is gone.

"I can't believe this," Marty said. "I haven't had a flat in six months, and now I get two at one time."

We had a jack and a lug wrench under the driver's seat, but we didn't have a spare tire. Which meant that we jacked up the buggy, took off the tires, and started a little game of roll the tire.

We left our fishing gear in the buggy, except for my creel with the fish in it. Then we each took a tire. The tires were too flat to roll straight and too big and heavy to carry easily, so we kept switching from one bad way to the other.

We'd gone about a mile when Marty spotted his father over on the next ridge. "Dad!" he yelled. "Hey, Dad!"

"Hey!" Mr. McNabb called back. I was plenty happy to see him. He was a big man, with arms the size of most people's legs. I figured he could carry both tires and still outrun Marty and me.

"We got two flat tires," Marty yelled.

"Too bad," Mr. McNabb answered.

"Will you help us?"

Mr. McNabb waved his arm. "You're big boys," he called, then turned and disappeared into the trees.

"It was a good thought," Marty said.

It was almost sundown by the time we got to Marty's place. We left the tires by the garage and drank about ten glasses of water. Then we collapsed on the ground.

"I just thought of something," Marty said after we'd rested awhile.

"First time for everything," I said.

"When we get those tires fixed, we have to haul them back up there."

"Won't your dad help?"

"You saw how much he helped today."

"I think I'm going to be busy this week," I said. "Really busy."

When I finally rode my bike home, Dad was cooking fish. "I couldn't wait any longer," he said. "But I weighed and measured mine before they went in the pan."

"How big was your biggest?"

"Thirty-eight inches long. And he weighed five pounds."

I looked into the pan at the two trout frying. With the heads off, they fit nicely in the pan. Twelve-inchers at the most.

"He had a very large head," Dad said. "Very heavy."

I took my three fish out of the creel and held them up. "What do you think?"

Dad shook his head. "Pitiful."

"You owe me ten cents," I said.

"No way," Dad said. "I can haul mine out of the pan right now. They still weigh more than yours."

"I'll get the scales."

He reached into his pocket and hauled out a dime. "I'm too hungry to argue with you. Put your tiny fish in the freezer and pour us some milk."

I got our milk and finished setting the table. "Where'd you catch your miniature fish?" I asked. "I want to know so that I don't waste my time going there."

"Foster Creek," he said. "Just down the road a couple miles."

The old surge ran up my arms.

I glanced over at Dad. He was draining the fish on a paper towel. He didn't seem to be joking.

"Where?" I asked.

"Foster Creek," he said. "Did you put the salt on the table?"

I turned to get the salt. But the surge was running up my arms again.

I couldn't believe it. Dad was lying to me.

It was a weird dinner. The trout were probably good, but I didn't notice. I just shoveled in food out of habit. When I couldn't stand the quiet any longer, I told Dad about Ricketts Lake and about the flat tires. And he made jokes about my tiny fish.

But I felt like I was talking to a stranger.

Eight

Every second Sunday morning Marty and his mother drove to Yreka for church. Afterward she bought groceries for the next two weeks, picked up whatever art supplies she needed, and visited with her friends and relatives. "I need a day in civilization now and then," she said.

I guess Marty's father didn't need much civilization. He almost never went along.

Unless Dad and I had something special planned, I went with Marty. Our favorite place in Yreka was the pizza parlor, where there were video games and, if we were lucky, some girls our age.

After the church service, Marty and I usually went straight to the pizza parlor to eat lunch and check out the scenery. That day, though, we had to stop at a tire store.

We hauled out the brush buggy tires, and a huge guy named Jim grabbed one in each hand. We could have used him up on the ridge.

It was fun to watch him work. He didn't waste a motion. In

no time, he put air into the tires, shoved them into a barrel of water, and marked the leaks. "I don't like the looks of these, boys," he said. "I think I'd better yank 'em off the rim."

"Is that gonna cost extra?" Marty asked.

Jim grinned. "Special price for you. A hundred bucks." In a minute, he had the tire off the metal rim. I looked inside and saw the jagged hole. "What'd you boys run over?"

"A rock, I guess," Marty said.

"Mighty funny rock." Jim set the tire aside. "Let's take a look at the other one." The other tire had the same kind of hole. "You got a matching pair, boys."

"Can you fix them?" Marty asked.

"No problem." Jim got out his patching supplies. "How'd this happen?"

"We don't know," I told him. "We were fishing. When we came back, the tires were flat."

Jim let out a whistle. "Somebody mad at you boys?"

I thought of Amos Lawlor, but Marty said, "No way."

"Don't be too sure," Jim said.

Marty leaned over and looked into the tire that hadn't been fixed yet. "You mean, somebody jammed a nail into our tire?"

"It's not that easy," Jim said. "You'd have to get a hammer and pound it in. But I don't think that's what happened here."

I ran my fingers over the jagged hole. "Then what did happen?"

"See how it's torn up there?" Jim said. "Looks like a corkscrew to me."

"That's crazy," I said. "Who'd have a corkscrew out in the hills?"

"Anybody with a Swiss Army knife," Jim said. "And that's half the guys in the county."

"That's crazy," Marty said. "Nobody would do that to us."

"Maybe," I said. After the week I'd had, I wasn't sure about anything.

After we loaded the tires into the van, Mrs. McNabb said she wanted me to talk to somebody. I was ready for lunch, but it was her van.

On the way, she told me about a book she'd been reading. She said a man in England used a forked stick—the same kind we used for water witching—to tell where old buildings once stood. And she told me about other creepy things, like one twin feeling pain when the other twin was hurt a thousand miles away.

We stopped in front of an old white house. "I want you to talk to Miriam," Mrs. McNabb said. "She's a gifted psychic."

I wasn't sure what a psychic was, but I caught on right away. Miriam was a pie-faced woman dressed in a flowery robe. She had weird music playing, and she kept nodding and smiling even when nothing was funny. Marty whispered to me that she used ESP and things like that. I thought maybe she was going to put on a show for us, but it turned out that I was supposed to be the show.

Miriam asked me to sit back in a recliner chair and close my eyes. "Breathe deeply," she said. "Relax."

But I couldn't relax at all. My chair smelled like smoky perfume, and I was sure that Marty was cracking up at the whole stupid thing.

Miriam shuffled a pack of cards, then asked, "Which card am I holding up?"

I couldn't get any kind of picture. "I'm sorry," I told her. "I can't do it."

"Just say whatever comes into your mind," she said. "Don't think. Don't try. Just say whatever comes."

So I did. "The eight of hearts."

"And the next one?" she asked.

We went through ten or twelve cards. I just named off whatever came into my head. I was kind of curious by then. As soon as Miriam said I could rest, I opened my eyes and looked toward Marty. "How'd I do?" I asked.

Marty shook his head. "Hundred percent. Missed every one."

Miriam tried other things—colors, numbers, shapes—but I was lousy at all of them. She didn't seem surprised, but Mrs. McNabb kept shaking her head. "There are many kinds of gifts," Miriam told me, taking my hand in both of hers. "Yours may be different from all others. You must follow it wherever it leads you."

When we went outside, Mrs. McNabb handed Miriam some money. "I'm sorry," I said when we got into the van. "I didn't mean to waste your money."

"Don't be silly," Mrs. McNabb said. "This was my idea. I was just curious." But she sounded disappointed.

Marty and I made our regular stop at the pizza parlor. We met a girl named Dorothy, who was kind of cute, except that she popped her gum with every chew. When she was leaving, she told us she had a steady boyfriend. By that time we'd heard her gum explode enough times that we weren't too brokenhearted.

When Mrs. McNabb picked us up from the pizza parlor, she said she needed to talk to her brother Ray. "My mother has a birthday coming up, and we've got to plan a party." Ray lived in Yreka, but that day he was at his new job—at the Agricultural Inspection Station north of town.

I didn't know much about the station, but Mrs. McNabb explained it to me. California has laws against bringing in fruit and plants from other places. The idea is to keep out plant diseases and insects.

When we got to the inspection station, Ray was handling the car lane. The way he was operating, I wasn't sure how much good he was doing. He'd ask drivers where they were coming from and whether they had any fresh fruits or plants. Then he'd give them a tourist magazine and wave them on through.

We parked the van off to the side, and he talked to us between cars. "Just hang on a few minutes. Harvey'll be back from his break right away."

A steady stream of cars came through. Ray asked the same questions over and over. Once, for no reason that I could see, he had a driver open his trunk.

"How'd you pick him?" I asked, once the driver was gone.

"He was acting weird," Ray said. "Probably feeling guilty about something. But he didn't have any fruit."

A few minutes later, a man in a red Mustang pulled up. Ray

asked the usual questions, and the man said that he came from Seattle and that he didn't have any fruit.

Suddenly I felt my arms twitch. The man was lying—I was sure of it.

"Ray," I said, just as he was handing the driver the magazine.

Ray turned toward me, looking a little peeved. "What's the matter?"

I moved up close to him and whispered, "Check his trunk."

Ray shrugged and turned back. "Would you open your trunk, please?"

"What for?" the driver asked.

"This is an agricultural inspection station," Ray said.

The driver got out and put his key in the trunk lock. Before he raised the lid, he turned to Ray and said, "All right, I've got a box of cherries in there. How was I supposed to know they were illegal?"

Marty slapped me on the back. "Way to go, Champ."

Ray took away the cherries, wrote down the man's name, and sent him off. By that time, a whole line of cars was backed up. When things settled down again, Ray called out, "Okay, Sam, how'd you know?"

I held out my hands. "I just did."

"This is a walking, talking lie detector," Marty said.

I listened to the drivers for a while but didn't get any twitches. Marty and I sat on the ground and ate cherries. Ray said we might as well. The cherries would be destroyed at the end of the day anyway.

Then, when I wasn't even watching close, I got the feeling

again. The car was a gray station wagon with an old couple in the front seat. "Ray," I said.

He looked over his shoulder. "You sure?"

I could feel the surge up my arms. "Positive."

As soon as Ray asked the couple to open the back of the station wagon, the woman remembered they had some bulbs from her sister's place in Idaho. Again Ray took away the stuff and sent them off.

"It's Magic Sam, the human lie detector," Marty said.

"You're something," Ray said to me. "You could have a big future in this business."

I felt great. Finally I'd found a way to do some good with my gift.

Ray took his break and sat in the van with Mrs. McNabb. Marty and I ate cherries and watched the cars come through the station. For a while we played a Miriam kind of game. We each guessed what make the tenth car would be. We each got two right out of twelve tries.

"We must follow our gift wherever it leads us," Marty said, sounding a little like Miriam. "And right now our gift is leading us down the tubes."

When Ray went back to work, Marty and I got a last handful of cherries. An old woman in a green Pontiac pulled up. When Ray asked her the usual two questions, she said, "I've been up to see my sister in Roseburg" and "No, sir."

But the surge ran up my arm, as strong as it had ever been.

"Ray," I said.

He looked back at me. "You're kidding."

"No," I said.

He shrugged and turned back to the woman. "Ma'am, I'd like to have you open your trunk for me."

"Certainly, sir." The woman stepped out of the car, marched back to the trunk, and raised the lid. The only thing in the trunk was the spare tire.

"I make this trip all the time," the woman said. "I know better than to try to bring in anything."

The surge ran up my arm again.

Ray looked at me and shrugged.

I stepped forward and whispered, "Check inside. She's got something."

Ray turned to the woman. "I'll need to look inside for a minute. It's no problem. It's just routine."

"I've been through here dozens of times," the woman said. "This has never happened before."

"We do it by numbers," Ray said. "This time you happened to be the hundredth car." He looked in the backseat, then bent over to look under the front seat. He stepped back and looked my way.

"I'd never try to take anything through," the woman said.

And again I felt the surge. I moved up next to Ray and whispered, "It's gotta be there."

Ray nodded. "I just need to check your glove box, ma'am, and you'll be out of here."

The woman let out a moan that was like a siren. "Oh, please don't arrest me," she burst out. "Please. I just got a couple of apples at the store. I didn't even think of them until I pulled in. Oh, please." She sagged against the car, tears running down her face.

"It's okay, ma'am," Ray said. "Commercial fruit like that is okay. You're fine."

"I've never done anything like this before," the woman sobbed.

"You can go, ma'am," Ray said. "No harm done."

But the woman just leaned against the car and cried.

"Please, ma'am," Ray said, taking her elbow and easing her into the car, "you're blocking the lane."

The woman finally started her engine and drove off, but she pulled to the side of the road about a hundred yards beyond the station.

"I'm sorry," I told Ray.

He waved me away. "People are nuts."

By then, Marty was caught up in the whole thing. Each time a new driver stopped, he asked me, "What about this one?"

But I was exhausted. I could barely keep my eyes open.

When we left, Ray shook hands with me. "You're something else, Sam. Come back anytime."

On the drive into Yreka, Marty made jokes about the kind of jobs I could get, and Mrs. McNabb wanted me to tell her exactly what I felt. But I was too tired to do much but hang my head out the window and let the wind blow my hair.

I was glad when we picked up Uncle Gene. That gave Mrs. McNabb somebody else to talk to. Or listen to. Uncle Gene was wound up like a clock. "Never stayed in a place like that in my life," he said. "Had a bed the size of my house."

"Did you win any money?" Marty asked him.

Uncle Gene turned in the seat and looked back at us. "I didn't fall for their trap. That's what it is, see? They get you over there and get you all fired up, and then they take your money. But not me. I didn't spend one red cent." He hauled his wallet out of his back pocket and showed us the fifty-dollar bill. "That's a lot of groceries, boys."

Pretty soon he was telling about all the things to eat at the hotel buffet. But I didn't listen. I was thinking of that old woman back at the inspection station. I slid down in the seat so that my head could rest on the back. That way, I didn't have to hold it up.

Nine

Whenever I went to Yreka, I brought Carmen something. Nothing big or fancy, just something stupid that we didn't have in Alder Creek. Green licorice, a rubber spider, wax vampire teeth. Once I even brought her a plastic cow that mooed when you turned it upside down.

That time I'd found some blackberry bubble gum.

Usually on those Monday mornings, Carmen would be waiting for me at the corner of the schoolyard. That Monday, though, she was turning the jump rope for some of the little kids. And she was carefully not looking in my direction.

Marty jogged over to me. "Hey, Sam," he said, "I hope you rested up. We've got to haul tires this afternoon."

"I can hardly wait." I looked over his shoulder toward Carmen, who was still turning the jump rope.

"She's mad," Marty said.

"What about?"

Marty shook his head. "Hey, you're asking the wrong guy. I

don't understand women. I don't understand girls either. I don't even understand female dogs."

"What happened?"

"Nothing. I was just telling her about how you picked out the liars at the inspection station, and all of a sudden she stomped off like I'd called her names."

"You weren't supposed to tell anybody," I said.

"Give me a break, Sam. Carmen doesn't count. You already told her about the lie detector stuff."

"And it was a mistake," I said. "All she did was get mad. And now she's mad at me all over again."

"I'm sorry," Marty said. "It was so neat I had to tell somebody."

"You want to do me a favor?"

"I know—keep my mouth shut."

"Besides that," I said. "How about turning a jump rope for a minute?"

Carmen and Aurelia were whipping the rope around while four little girls jumped together. Marty moved up beside Carmen, put his hand on the rope, and said, "My turn." He took over the rope without breaking the rhythm.

Carmen turned toward me, then looked away.

"Have you been a good girl?" I asked her.

"Not particularly."

"I brought you a present anyway." I handed her the blackberry gum.

"Thank you." She still didn't look at me.

One of the jumpers caught her foot in the rope, and they had to start over. "Somebody else can turn it," Marty said.

"No, no," the little girls yelled. And in a second Marty and

Aurelia had the rope going again, and the little ones were skipping and chanting, "Little yellow ducky swimming in the stream."

"I hate to make you miss 'Little Yellow Ducky,' " I said, "but could we talk for a minute?"

We walked slowly across the playground. I was hoping she'd start, but she outwaited me. Finally I said, "I know you're mad, but I don't know why."

"I'm not mad."

"Well, if you're happy, you're doing a good job of hiding it."

Carmen stopped walking and looked at me. "I don't like what you're doing. It's scary."

"It's not like I'm trying to do it," I said. "It just happens."

"How do you think it makes me feel? I'm afraid to talk to you."

"Come on."

"What if I say I like your shirt? Something like that. And then you start getting your zaps, so you think I'm lying to you."

"Take it easy," I told her. "I know you won't lie to me."

"I might," she said. "Maybe I don't want to hurt your feelings. Or maybe something is none of your business."

"What's wrong with my shirt?" I asked her, trying to change the subject.

"Don't you see?" Carmen went on. "It doesn't help to know if somebody's lying unless you know why they're doing it."

Mrs. McNabb came outside and blew the whistle that meant school was starting. I was just as glad. That conversation wasn't going anywhere.

"Thanks for the gum," Carmen said. "Do you think it'll turn my mouth purple?"

"Give a piece to your little brother and find out."

Right after school I went home and got my bike and my backpack. Then I rode over to the store to get a six-pack of root beer. It was going to be a long trip up the ridge with the tires.

Amos Lawlor's pickup was parked by the gas pump, and I saw him sitting on a bench. I was a little scared, but I didn't think he'd say anything to me with other people around.

Uncle Gene was walking up and down the porch, and Dr. Vincent, wearing his khaki shorts and Smokey hat, was leaning against the railing. Mrs. Lopez stood in the doorway.

"It was a burglar," Uncle Gene was shouting.

"But he didn't take nothing?" Lawlor asked.

"It was probably a squirrel or a rat," Dr. Vincent said.

"I can tell the difference between a squirrel and a burglar," Uncle Gene said. "And this was a burglar. He went through all my stuff. Probably thought I'd never know the difference."

"What's going on?" I asked.

Lawlor gave me a rotten look and turned away.

"The whole thing was a trick," Uncle Gene said. "I knew there was something fishy about that Reno business. They wanted to get me outa the way. Then they came in and searched the place."

"What's missing?" I asked.

Uncle Gene smiled for the first time. "Not a thing, boy. I know better than to leave things lying around. You know what they was after, don't you?"

"All your fancy furniture and dishes maybe," Dr. Vincent said with a smile.

"Smart aleck," Uncle Gene said to him. "They was after my maps. But I fooled 'em good." He let out a laugh.

"Who?" I asked.

"The guys after my stuff," Uncle Gene said. "It's easy to hide stuff when you got a log cabin. You take off a log and hollow out a space, and there's your hideout. Put the log back, and a guy could look for a week and not find it."

"Could have been some kids messing around," Mrs. Lopez said, giving me the eye.

"Listen, it wasn't me," I told her. "I was fishing at Ricketts Lake on Saturday, and I was in Yreka yesterday."

"Sam wouldn't do me that way," Uncle Gene said, putting his hand on my shoulder.

"I still think it was an animal," Dr. Vincent said. "Nobody'd go clear out there to look through your stuff."

"That's how much you know," Uncle Gene said. "Those maps are worth plenty, and some people around here are smart enough to know it."

Dr. Vincent laughed.

"You think you're so smart," Uncle Gene said. "There's a guy in town here paying me good money just for a little share of what I find."

I expected a surge to run up my arms, but it didn't.

"Who?" Mrs. Lopez asked.

"Never mind," Uncle Gene told her. "But that guy'll end up a rich man. You just wait."

"Yeah," Dr. Vincent said, "I figure we'll have a gold rush any day now."

I went inside, bought my root beer, and stuffed it into the backpack. I thought about the people in town, trying to come up with somebody besides Uncle Gene who might believe in the maps. I couldn't think of a single possibility.

Carmen was waiting for me outside her house. "I'll go with you," she said. "I figure you guys can use all the help you can get." So she rode along beside me, her head bent over the handlebars.

While I was swinging the McNabbs' gate open, Carmen said, "Look," and stuck out her tongue. It was a horrible purple color.

It took me a second to remember about the blackberry gum. Then I said, "You look like you have a disease."

"Maybe I'm allergic to mind readers."

When we got to the cabin, we saw Mrs. McNabb at her easel. Some half-grown ducks were keeping her company this time. We waved and rode on by. Marty was in the backyard with the tires. "Carmen," he said, "thanks for coming. Sam needs some help."

"Me?" I said. "You're the one who almost died getting the tires down here."

"Don't worry," Carmen said. "I don't plan on working. I just came along to watch you suffer."

We started out with Carmen carrying the backpack and Marty and me rolling the tires. It was tough keeping my tire rolling uphill. A couple of times it just about got away from me, and I had to flop it on its side so that it wouldn't roll back downhill. By the time we'd gone a quarter mile, Carmen traded with me. And soon after that, I traded with Marty.

Along the way we met Marty's father. He had a huge

backpack with bare sticks and old deer antlers poking out the top. With that pack and his bushy beard, he made me think of Santa Claus.

"You guys having a lot of fun?" he called out.

"Sure," I said.

"Hi, Mr. McNabb," Carmen said. "What do you have in there?"

"Treasures," he said. "Genuine treasures."

"If you offered to help us," Marty told him, "it wouldn't make us mad."

Mr. McNabb smiled and shook his head. "I wouldn't spoil your fun."

"Please, Dad—" Marty began.

Mr. McNabb cut him off. "If you're big enough to drive, you're big enough to take care of the problems." He didn't sound mean or anything, but that ended the conversation.

"Happy treasure hunting," Carmen called out as he walked off. A minute later she asked Marty, "What does he do with that junk?"

Marty smiled. "He makes sculptures and stuff. Right now he's collecting stuff for a Bigfoot thing he's making out of barbed wire and old wood."

"Do people really buy stuff like that?" I asked.

"You don't make sculptures to sell," Marty said. "You make 'em because you feel like it. Then when you're done, you see if anybody wants to buy 'em."

"You think anybody will?" I asked.

Marty shrugged. "You know somebody that wants a fourteen-foot-tall Bigfoot?"

The next time I had the backpack, I told them about Uncle

Gene and the burglar. They couldn't make any more sense out of it than I could.

When we stopped to drink a root beer, Marty sat down on his tire and looked at me. "Sam, do you think there was a burglar?"

"Uncle Gene thinks so," I said. "And he ought to know."

"I was thinking about these tires," Marty said.

"Me too."

"What's going on?" Carmen asked.

"Funny stuff," I said. "The guy at the tire store said that these flats weren't an accident, that somebody punched holes in the tires."

"You didn't tell me that," she said.

"So, just say Uncle Gene's right," I went on. "If somebody wanted to make sure we didn't go down to Uncle Gene's cabin and catch them there, all they had to do was zap our tires."

"But it's crazy," Marty said. "Who'd go to that kind of trouble for some dumb maps?"

We talked about it off and on for the next hour, but we didn't get any further.

"I know how we can do it," Carmen said finally. "We'll get all the suspects in a room, and then the mind reader here can figure out who did it."

We all laughed, but I had to fake mine. I'd been thinking the same thing.

By the time we got to the brush buggy, all three of us were dragging. Before we put on the tires, we flopped down on the ground and shared the last root beer, which was pretty warm by then. But it still tasted great.

"I'm glad I don't have ESP," Carmen said. "The last half

hour I kept having this horrible feeling that we'd get up here and find the other two tires flat."

"Don't talk that way until we're safe in my yard," Marty said.

Carmen rubbed the muscles in her legs. "You guys owe me. A lot."

"I'll make it up to you," I told her. "Next time I'm in Yreka I'll buy you *two* packs of blackberry bubble gum."

"In that case, I can afford to be generous." She hauled out her gum and gave us each a piece. We sat there on the tires and blew purple bubbles. Then we had an ugly tongue contest, and we were all winners.

Carmen and I had a biggest-bubble contest while Marty put the tires on the buggy. I won two out of three and ended up with gum in my eyebrows.

Since there are only two seats in the buggy, Carmen had to sit on my lap for the trip back. Life is tough sometimes.

That night I cooked the three trout I'd caught on Saturday. "It's a good thing you brought home extras," Dad said. "Two of yours are the size of one of mine."

At dinner I told him about Uncle Gene and the burglar. "You think those maps are worth anything?" I asked him.

Dad shrugged. "They're worth a lot to Uncle Gene. A guy needs a dream."

"Is it just a dream? Isn't there gold still left around here?"

He smiled. "Depends how you look at it. Almost any creek you pick, you can find a little color. When Uncle Gene is panning instead of looking for lost mines, he can make four, five dollars a day."

"But I mean real money. Don't you think there's a chance he could hit it big?"

Dad shrugged. "About the same chance as being hit by lightning, I guess."

"Somebody must think there's a chance," I said. "Today Uncle Gene told Dr. Vincent that he has a secret partner. Somebody's paying Uncle Gene for a share of what he finds."

Dad pushed his chair back from the table. "Somebody else has a dream, I guess."

I got up and stacked the dishes. "I can't figure who it could be. Who'd want to be Uncle Gene's secret partner?"

"Could be anybody but you and me," Dad said. "A lot of people get bit by the gold bug. Those maps look worthless to us, but maybe somebody sees something we don't."

While he was talking, a surge ran up my arms. I almost dropped the dishes I was carrying. I looked over my shoulder at Dad, but he was just gathering up the silverware. I couldn't remember exactly what he'd said, but something there had set me off.

"Do you have homework tonight?" he asked.

"Mrs. McNabb doesn't give us much," I said.

"Good. You get to do the dishes then."

It took me a long time to clean up. I kept trying to remember exactly what Dad had said. And I kept thinking about that old woman crying at the inspection station.

It should have been a good night. I'd had a buggy ride with Carmen snuggled on my lap, and I'd been co-champion of the ugly tongue contest. But I couldn't get comfortable. Something weird was going on, and Dad seemed to be smack in the middle of it.

Ten

Every time I went to the store, somebody was lying about their dog or their car or their kids. You name it, the Alder Creek people lied about it.

One afternoon I listened to some men talk about snakes. Perfect score—I got surges on every single story. I could understand that, I guess. Maybe you needed to jazz up a snake story.

But Mrs. Cavalo lied about getting stains out of a dress, and Mrs. Lopez lied about what her cat ate, and Frank Caldwell lied about his chain saw.

It was disgusting. After a while I didn't want to listen to people. When I needed something at the store, I rushed in and rushed out.

After school on Thursday Mrs. McNabb took Marty, Carmen, Aurelia, and me over to Elk Meadow. It should have been a two-hour drive, but she stopped her van every two minutes so Uncle Gene could point at some bare hillside or ratty shack and tell us about a mine or lumber camp that used to be there.

The Elk Meadow school was having a program about the history of the town. Mrs. McNabb hoped we could do the same kind of program for Alder Creek. She brought Uncle Gene along because he knew more about our area than anybody else. Dad said it best: "Uncle Gene remembers everything, whether it happened or not."

Uncle Gene didn't want to go. He was worried about burglars. But Mrs. McNabb said she'd buy him dinner at the steakhouse in Elk Meadow. So we all got to eat in a fancy restaurant, and Uncle Gene put away a steak so big it hung over the sides of his plate. I ordered fried oysters. They were kind of chewy but I didn't care. No MOTSOT for me. I wanted to eat something I'd never had in my life.

The program was kind of interesting. The students gave reports on things like logging and fishing, and old people told about the early days. And Marty met a girl named Tracy, who gave a boring report on mining but who had gorgeous brown eyes.

Uncle Gene kept muttering "Yep, that's right" all through the kids' reports. When the old people talked, he got even louder. That wouldn't have been so bad except that he was saying things like "She's got that all wrong" and "Nope, that's not how it was."

When the program was over, Uncle Gene stayed right by the main table, putting away cookies while he argued with a woman about the name of a mine. Marty got Tracy's phone number, which wasn't going to do him much good. It was a big-money toll call, and Marty didn't even have a phone.

We tried to sleep on the way home, but those roads aren't built for sleeping and Uncle Gene was jawing away the whole time. It was past eleven when they dropped me at my house. I staggered straight to my bedroom, slid out of my clothes, and collapsed into bed.

I must have slept for over an hour, but it seemed like just a few seconds before the fire bell started to clang.

I threw off the covers and yanked on my clothes, then raced out the front door and climbed into the pickup with Dad. Two of the neighbors drove past before we could back into the road.

Pickups with their lights on were sitting in front of the store. Somebody was backing the fire truck out of its garage. Dr. Vincent, who's the fire chief, was up on the porch calling out orders: "Ray, Dennis—some of you guys with pickups— you can outrun the truck. Grab some backpumps and get out there right away. We'll be along as soon as we can."

"Where is it?" Dad shouted.

"Gaither's place," somebody said.

"Uncle Gene's house is on fire," someone else yelled.

I saw Uncle Gene standing beside Dr. Vincent. He was waving his arms and yelling, but I couldn't hear what he was saying.

A pickup tore away from the store and another one followed. "We might as well go along," Dad said. We headed down the road a lot faster than he usually drives, but the lights ahead of us got smaller and smaller.

We were about half a mile away before I spotted the orange glow. By then, we were bouncing through washed-out ruts down to Uncle Gene's clearing. "Looks good," Dad said. "It hasn't gotten into the trees."

I kept my eyes on that glow while the pickup bumped along the chewed-up road. I cinched down my seatbelt to keep from banging my head on the roof. "I'm glad I'm not driving the fire truck," Dad muttered.

Dad left the pickup beside the corral, and we jumped out and ran uphill. Only one wall was still standing, and flames were running up both sides of it. The rest of the cabin had caved in, and most of the logs were bright orange embers. Some of the men were already circling the fire with their backpump units.

Uncle Gene's outhouse, which was about twenty yards back of the cabin, was still standing. Two men were squirting water on the roof and the outer walls to keep them from catching fire.

Mr. and Mrs. Lopez were in the back of their pickup, handing out backpumps. Mr. Lopez gave one to Dad. "Not much to do," he said.

"Looks like it'll burn straight to the ground," Dad said. "That'll make clean-up easier."

I grabbed a backpump and slid my arms through the straps. "That's pretty heavy," Mr. Lopez said. I waved him away and started off. He was right, of course. The outfit weighed a good sixty pounds. The cold metal tank dug into my back, and the water in the tank sloshed with each step I took. I tried not to stagger while I sprayed water on a few smoldering sticks.

Amos Lawlor backed into me. Our backpumps clanged

together. "Always gettin' in my way, ain't you?" he said. I moved away without looking at him.

When I couldn't find anything else to spray, I stood around with the men and watched the fire polish off the cabin. It was beautiful—bright orange coals with yellow and blue flames shooting out—until I remembered what I was watching.

By the time the fire truck pulled into the yard, the last wall was sagging. "Back it around," Dr. Vincent shouted. "Unroll the hoses."

Uncle Gene climbed down from the fire truck and walked straight toward the burning cabin. For a second I thought he was going to walk into the flames. But he stopped a few feet away and just stood there shaking his head.

"Better get back, Uncle Gene," somebody yelled. "You'll singe your eyebrows."

Dad trotted over to Dr. Vincent. "Might as well let it burn," he yelled.

The men unrolled the hoses and started soaking down everything around there. We hadn't had a fire in a long time, and everybody wanted a turn with the hoses. Besides, Dr. Vincent figured they couldn't get the fire truck back up that road until the tank was empty.

When I looked around again, Uncle Gene was gone. I walked around a little but didn't see him anywhere.

Pretty soon the men turned the hoses on the cabin for a minute. "We don't want it to get too hot," Dr. Vincent said. Everybody liked hearing the sizzle when the water hit the fire. Big clouds of smoke and steam rose up.

"Little boys playing with their toys," Mrs. Lopez said.

When most of the water was gone, we stood around and

watched the flames. The night was chilly, so people got up close enough to stay warm.

Pretty soon I saw Uncle Gene walking around on the far side of the fire truck. I walked over there and asked, "You okay, Uncle Gene?"

He reached out and messed up my hair. "Well, boy, it's kind of a rough night." He looked out into the darkness. "Can't find Leonard and the sheep. Fire must have scared them. They knocked down the fence and took off."

"I'm sorry, Uncle Gene," I said.

"Oh, he'll be back in the morning."

I was talking about his house, not Leonard, but I let it go.

When Uncle Gene came back to the fire, somebody called out, "You got any marshmallows, Gene?"

"This ain't funny," Uncle Gene said. "This is mean business." He started marching up and down, walking between us and the fire. He didn't seem to notice the heat. "If I hadn't been gone, they'd have got me. I'd be a dead man right now."

"Who?" somebody asked him. "Who was it?"

"The burglars," Uncle Gene said. "They sent me to Reno so they could go after my maps. Then they tried to kill me."

Some of the men looked away to hide their smiles.

"Come on, Gene," one man said. "No burglar could find his way out here."

"What's he talking about?" somebody else wanted to know.

"They woulda burned me up in my bed," Uncle Gene said. "I'm lucky to be alive."

Mrs. Lopez said out loud what I'd been thinking: "If somebody wanted those maps, why would they start a fire and burn them up?"

"But they didn't get 'em," Uncle Gene said to nobody in particular. "They burned down my house, but they didn't get my maps. I outsmarted 'em."

"Who?" somebody asked. "Who are you talking about?"

"Sounds pretty farfetched to me," somebody else said.

"I don't care what you think," Uncle Gene shouted. "They were after me. They wanted to kill me!"

Nobody argued with him. The last of his house was disappearing into a pile of orange coals. He could say anything he wanted.

Slowly people began to drift away. Dr. Vincent and some other men said they'd spend the night, but there was nothing for anybody to do. Dad and I put our backpump units with the others and headed for the pickup.

It was cold in the cab of the truck. I curled into a ball with my arms wrapped tight against my chest. "What'll Uncle Gene do now?" I asked.

"He'll be all right," Dad said. "They were talking about getting a trailer in here for him. And Mrs. Lopez will collect stuff for him at the store."

The heater in the pickup gradually warmed up. If I could have quit bouncing, I would have gone to sleep. "Dad," I said, "do you think somebody set that fire?"

"No," he said. "I think it was an accident."

The old surge ran up my arms. Dad was lying again.

Eleven

At school the next morning everybody was talking about the fire. Marty was disgusted about missing the whole thing. "Living out where we do," he said, "the world could come to an end, and we'd find out about it two days later."

Carmen had gotten dressed when she heard the fire bell, but her father wouldn't let her go. "Isn't that stupid?" she said. "Because I'm a girl, I'm supposed to stay home and let the big tough men go fight the fire."

"Don't worry," I said. "I took care of it for you."

She smacked me on the arm. "Don't start with me. I'm mad. There wasn't a reason in the world for me not to go. I could fight a fire just as well as you could. It's about time women's lib got to Alder Creek."

"My mother went to the fire," Aurelia told Carmen.

"That's a start," Carmen said.

"But I had to stay home and take care of my little brother," Aurelia finished.

"Fortunately for you," I said, "your reporter was on the

scene." I went ahead and told them the whole story, laying it on a little heavy about how I used the backpump.

Of course, I didn't tell what I'd been thinking about all morning—Dad. Funny things were going on. Dad had lied about Saturday. That didn't mean he was the burglar, but he wasn't ruled out either. And he knew something about Uncle Gene's business that he was hiding. But what did that mean? And he'd been alone last night. He could have gone out to Uncle Gene's and set the fire. But what possible reason could he have?

None of it made sense.

Mrs. McNabb went into action right away. Her first idea, as soon as she heard about the fire, was to take the bus out there. When she found out the road was too rough for that, she started calling parents. By nine o'clock she'd located two other people with vans.

She was worried about the little kids getting scared, so she had one older student go in each van. That way, we could keep the little ones calmed down. I don't know what happened in the other vans, but the boys in mine told stupid jokes and had burping contests. As soon as we got to Uncle Gene's, they all lined up by the fire and spit into it. They liked to hear their spit sizzle.

The fire had died down to a pile of smoking ashes. Once in a while a coal would pop or a flame would shoot up, but it was like a big campfire. Since most of the kids had never seen Uncle Gene's place, they could hardly get the idea of what had happened.

Billy Cavalo had to go to the bathroom, so we pointed him toward the outhouse. He opened the door and started to cough. "It's poison gas," he yelled. He took some big breaths and then rushed in, holding his nose. As soon as he came out, half the other boys claimed they had to go. And we had more coughing and choking and nose-holding.

The fire truck was still there, but the hoses were rolled up and stored away. Dr. Vincent came over and started lecturing us about fire and the danger of playing with matches. Bobby Keck raised his hand and asked, "Was Uncle Gene playing with matches?"

We'd been there about half an hour when Uncle Gene marched into the clearing with Leonard and the sheep following him. "Stay back, kids," he shouted. "Leonard's skittery today." That suited everybody fine.

After Uncle Gene had led the animals into the corral and given them some hay from the shed, he came up and let the little ones pat his beard. "I'm sorry your house burned down," Jenny Cavalo said.

"Where you gonna live, Uncle Gene?" Bobby Keck asked him.

"I guess I'll have to crawl under a bush," Uncle Gene said. None of the kids laughed.

"I hope you don't have to live in the outhouse," Luther said, and everybody gave him a dirty look.

Bobby Keck's eyes were shiny, and Amy Ricketts was sniffing. "You can live with us," Billy Cavalo said. "We got lots of room."

Dr. Vincent got out one of the backpumps and let the kids

try it out. While that was going on, Marty and I walked toward the fire with Uncle Gene. "I'm really sorry," Marty told him.

"Don't you worry about it," Uncle Gene said. "Wait'll you see the house I build after I locate the mine."

"Yeah," I said, trying to sound like I believed it.

"I'm getting close," Uncle Gene said. "That's why the guy done this. He knows I'm just about to find it. He was trying to get me out of the way."

That didn't sound any crazier than the explanations I could come up with.

"One thing I'm sorry about," Uncle Gene went on. "Wish I'd took a picture of the old place. Here I am carryin' that Polaroid camera everywhere, and I never did take a picture of my own house."

When the little kids got bored with the fire, Marty and I led everybody up the hill to the mine shaft. Mrs. McNabb said that nobody was to go inside, but most of the kids sneaked in for a minute. Then we went on a nature walk down to the creek and everybody collected tadpoles.

Mrs. McNabb kept checking her watch, so I knew something was up. Then we heard the blast of an air horn and saw Mr. Lopez's truck inching its way down the hill. Bouncing along behind it was a little silver trailer.

"Here it comes," Mrs. McNabb shouted. "The people of Alder Creek are bringing a new home for Uncle Gene."

I recognized the trailer right away. For the past year it had been sitting empty on a lot down the road from us. But to the little kids, the whole thing was magic.

To make things even better, Guido Cavalo followed behind in Uncle Gene's Jeep. The Jeep was piled high with boxes of things that people had collected for Uncle Gene—sheets, blankets, dishes, canned food.

"This is the kind of town you live in," Mrs. McNabb said. "Uncle Gene's been helping people all his life. And now when he needs help, everybody pitches in and helps him."

Uncle Gene got all choked up. "This is something," he muttered. "This is something."

For once, I was proud of Alder Creek—even if it was full of liars.

After Mr. Lopez put the trailer where Uncle Gene wanted it, the men who'd been there all night tried to get the trailer level. The language got hot in a hurry.

"You're doing it all wrong," one man yelled, tossing in a few extra words that made the little kids giggle.

"Nobody asked you," another one yelled back. "If you know so much, go ahead and do it yourself." Then he added some more words that kept the giggles going.

"Your mom's right," I whispered to Marty. "This'll show the kids what kind of town we've got. We help each other out, but we cuss each other while we're doing it."

Marty shrugged. "If you're in trouble and a guy's helping you, who cares if he cusses?"

While Mrs. McNabb was getting everybody loaded into the vans, Uncle Gene started to yell. He'd just found out that nobody had called the sheriff. "This wasn't no accident," he yelled. "I told you that."

"I'll call when I get home," Dr. Vincent told him.

"I want it done now," Uncle Gene shouted. "You, Sam, call up the sheriff as soon as you get to town. You tell him I want Deputy Bates sent up here right now."

"I'll call," Dr. Vincent said again.

"Sam'll take care of it." Uncle Gene pointed a finger at me. "You tell him to send Bates. And tell him to get me the hundred dollars he owes me too. I can use it right now, with all my stuff wiped out."

When we got to Alder Creek, I had them drop me at my house so that I could call the sheriff. I was put on hold twice. Then Deputy Bates came on the line. I told him about the fire and said that Uncle Gene wanted him to come out right away.

Bates laughed. "The old coot figures somebody did it on purpose, huh?"

"That's right," I said.

"Who'd do something like that?" he asked.

I didn't have an answer for that one.

Twelve

Back at school, we were supposed to write about the fire, but I was too tired to put much on paper. Besides, what could you say about seeing somebody's home wiped out? It was great that the people of the town had gotten Uncle Gene a new home, but one of those same people had burned down the old one.

I looked around and saw that nobody else was doing much writing either. After a while Mrs. McNabb gave up and let us go outside.

Carmen, Marty, and I wandered away from the others. "Is Deputy Bates coming?" Carmen asked me.

"I don't think so. He figures it was an accident."

"That's what everybody's saying," Marty said.

Carmen snorted. "Grown-ups drive me nuts. They know it was no accident."

"The whole thing's crazy," I said. "Who'd burn down his cabin?"

Carmen looked me straight in the eye. "You think it *was* an accident?"

"No, I think somebody did it. But I can't think of anybody with a reason."

Marty shook his head. "I can't think of anybody who'd do something that rotten even if they had a reason."

"I can," I said. "Amos Lawlor. He's rotten enough. But I don't know why he'd do it."

"I have an idea," Carmen said. "You can get some use out of your lie-detecting magic. Go up to Lawlor and ask him if he burned down Uncle Gene's house. Then, when he says no, you can tell if he's lying."

"Only one problem," I said. "He'd probably answer by punching me in the nose."

We stood and watched the little kids playing Red Light, Green Light. "You know what's gonna happen?" Carmen said. "Nothing. Nobody around here's gonna do a thing. And whoever set that fire will get away with it. Unless—" She stopped and smiled at us.

"Unless what?" I said.

"Unless we do something about it."

"Junior detectives to the rescue," Marty said.

"Don't laugh," Carmen said. "It's worth a try. We could ask a few questions anyway."

Marty grabbed the front of my shirt. "Excuse me, sir. Have you committed arson lately?"

"I'm serious," Carmen said. "At least we should talk to Uncle Gene. I'd like to go back out there anyway. We can take him a housewarming gift for his new trailer."

"He's had all the housewarming he needs," Marty said.

Carmen groaned. "Bad joke."

"What kind of gift?" I asked.

"We've got a bunch of cactus plants over at the house," she said. "I'll put one in a little pot. It'll be perfect for Uncle Gene. You can forget to water it for a month and it still does fine."

After school I went home and got my bike. On my way over to Carmen's, I stopped by the store and bought a box of gingersnaps. I didn't know what Uncle Gene thought about cactus, but I knew he loved gingersnaps.

When Carmen spotted me, she waved me on and yelled, "Let's roll." In her hand was a flowerpot the size of a paper cup. Once we were riding side by side, she said, "Mom's not home, so I left her a note. I wanted to get out of there before she came back and thought of some job I should be doing."

Marty was backing the buggy out of the barn when we rode up. Mr. McNabb waved to us and walked over to the buggy. He reached down and turned off the motor. "I didn't hear you ask permission."

Marty just smiled. "Is it okay if we go see Uncle Gene for a minute? We want to take him a present for his new place."

Mr. McNabb looked up at the mountains, then checked his watch. "All right, but I want you back here by 4:30."

"That's only an hour," Marty said. "We have to walk all the way down into the canyon and back."

"Five o'clock, and that's it." Mr. McNabb turned and walked toward the house.

Marty started the engine. Carmen and I climbed into the other seat and buckled the seatbelt around us. We sat side by side, both of us hanging over the edge.

With that engine roaring, we didn't try to talk until we stopped on the ridge above Uncle Gene's place. "That was weird back there," Marty said. "I usually tell him where I'm going, but I don't ask permission. And he doesn't set time limits."

Carmen waved him away. "You want to trade parents, let me know."

Halfway down the hill we started calling to Uncle Gene, but he didn't answer. We stopped by the corral and yelled again. Leonard was eyeing us, so we didn't stay there long.

"Maybe Uncle Gene's asleep," Marty said. "He was up all night."

We walked over by the trailer. I saw that somebody had hooked up the water line. Probably with a big supply of arguing and cussing.

"I'll put the plant inside," Carmen said. She climbed up the two steps and tried the knob. "It's locked. I can leave it on the steps, I guess."

"Howdy, kids," Uncle Gene called out. He stepped out from behind the trailer. I was pretty sure he'd been there the whole time.

That bothered me. We'd been with him in Elk Meadow the night before, so he knew we couldn't have started the fire. But after what had happened, he didn't trust anybody, not even his friends.

"Hi, Uncle Gene," Carmen said. "We brought you a plant for your new home." She handed him the cactus.

Uncle Gene turned the cactus one way, then the other. "That's something," he said, his voice shaking a little. "That's real nice."

"And some gingersnaps," I said, pushing the box toward him. "You gotta have gingersnaps in your new place."

Uncle Gene took the box in his free hand, then laughed. "Now how am I gonna get my key outa my pocket?" He handed me the cookies and reached for his key. He unlocked the door and pushed it back. "Go right in, young lady."

Once all three of us were inside, he squeezed in and slammed the door. The trailer was neat. It had a little stove and sink and a table with a bench on each side. The only thing it didn't have was room for four people. Marty and I slid onto the benches to get out of the way.

"Isn't this something?" Uncle Gene said. "It's even got a refrigerator. Works on propane. The guys lit it for me before they left." He shook his head. "Doesn't make any sense when you think about it. You burn up propane, and it makes things cold. But it works. So I got some cold juice for you kids." He opened a refrigerator that was about the size of a TV set and took out a can of punch. Then he dug into the cupboard and pulled out some glasses.

Carmen grabbed the glasses and rinsed them. "I can't believe you've got so many things put away already, Uncle Gene."

"Gotta do something," he said. "Too nervous to sleep. Can't even sit down very long."

Carmen poured four glasses of punch and set them on the table. Then she slid in beside me, and Uncle Gene sat next to Marty. "Here's to your new home," Carmen said, and we all clinked glasses. The punch wasn't all that cold, but Uncle Gene drained his and banged down the glass.

"I shoulda had a refrigerator a long time ago."

"You'd better have some more, Uncle Gene." Carmen poured him another glass.

Uncle Gene drank a little punch, then looked at me. "I'm still waitin' for the sheriff."

"I called him as soon as I got back to town. Ended up talking to Deputy Bates."

Uncle Gene shook his head. "He probably figures it was an accident."

"Probably," Marty muttered.

Uncle Gene slapped the table. "How could it be an accident? Fires don't start by themselves. My stove was out. And I don't have no electricity. And there wasn't no lightning. So how'd it start?"

We all shook our heads.

"People don't listen." Uncle Gene stood up, banging his knee on the stove. He rubbed the knee and said, "Things are a little tight in here." He backed up a step and leaned against the sink. "I told those melonheads there was a burglar at my place and they just laughed. And now the guy burned down my house and they say it was an accident."

"You want some more punch, Uncle Gene?" Carmen asked.

"I want people to listen!"

"We're listening," Carmen said. "Who could have done it?"

"Anybody!" Uncle Gene shouted. "They want to get that mine before I do!"

"But who?" Carmen asked. "Has someone been asking a lot of questions?"

"Amos Lawlor, maybe," I suggested.

Uncle Gene shook his head. "Could be anybody. That mine's worth millions."

Carmen tried a few more questions, but Uncle Gene kept coming back to the maps and the mine.

Finally Marty said, "This is a nice trailer, Uncle Gene."

Uncle Gene smiled. "Real nice. Got everything I need. But I'll tell you right now—I'm not about to sleep in here. That guy could come back anytime and set this one on fire too. And I don't even have my shotgun. It got burned up."

"What'll you do?" Carmen asked, pouring him another glass of punch.

"Gonna sleep out under the stars," he said. "I'm not givin' the guy another chance." He took a drink and set his glass on the table. "I'd be dead, and those melonheads would probably say it was an accident."

When we got up to leave, Uncle Gene remembered the gingersnaps. He wouldn't let us go until we each took a handful. "And I'll take real good care of that cactus," he told Carmen.

"Just water it every week or two," she said. "It'll be fine."

He walked with us down past the corral. "You kids are the best," he said, and his voice started to crack. "The best there is anywhere." A tear ran down his cheek and got lost in his beard.

We all stood there with our mouths open. He turned and headed for the hay shed. Leonard and the sheep came running. He hauled out some hay and dumped it over the fence for them. We yelled good-bye and headed uphill, keeping our eyes straight ahead.

On the way back, Carmen and I were seatbelted together again. After Marty checked the time, he went tearing down the ridge, bouncing us all over. "Not so fast," I yelled.

"Don't worry about your father," Carmen shouted. "If you don't slow down, I'll kill you before he gets a chance."

About a mile along, we were headed up a little rise, and I caught a glimpse of something blue in a patch of brush where nothing blue should have been. "Hold it!" I shouted.

Marty slowed a little. "What's the matter?"

I pointed to the brake pedal and worked my foot up and down. Marty shoved in the clutch and braked to a stop.

I whispered into Carmen's ear, "I think somebody's down in the brush."

Carmen passed the message on to Marty, and I pointed where I'd seen the flash.

I unbuckled the seatbelt, then slid out of the seat and headed downhill toward an open spot. Marty drove the buggy over the hill.

I saw the flash of blue again, then once more. Somebody was moving through the brush, toward the ridge. I got a fix on a pine tree that was about where he'd come out, then hurried down the ridge road.

By the time I got close to the pine, I could hear him crashing through the brush. I thought about hiding, but I was fifty feet from any cover except the lone tree. So I stood there and waited, my stomach sinking.

Below me, I could see a dark head bobbing above the manzanita bushes and sometimes a flash of blue shirt. I stood in the road, ready to run.

Then the brush parted, and a man stepped out into the clearing.

I smiled and let out the breath I'd been holding. "Hi, Mr. McNabb," I called out.

He jumped back.

"I'm sorry," I said. "I didn't mean to scare you."

He put a hand over his heart. "Sam," he said, shaking his head, "you did a number on me that time."

"I'm sorry," I said again.

He kept his hand on his chest as he came up the hill. He stopped a few feet from me and took a long breath. "Oh, well, what's a little heart attack among friends? How come you're not with Marty?"

"He's just down the road," I said. "What are you doing?"

"Treasure hunting," he said, pointing at his backpack.

I felt the surge run up my arms. He was lying.

I was too surprised to do anything but stare at him. Then I mumbled, "I'd better go," and headed away.

"See you, Sam," he said. "But next time, make a little noise, will you? My heart's still pounding."

I jogged over the hill to where Marty and Carmen were waiting beside the buggy.

"What was it?" he called out.

"It was just your dad," I said.

Marty broke into a smile. "That's good. I was worried there for a minute." He turned toward the buggy.

"He said he was looking for treasure."

Marty stopped and looked over his shoulder. "And did your famous lie detector alarm go off?"

The question caught me by surprise. Before I could think of an answer, he said, "Forget it. I can tell by the stupid look on your face."

"I don't know what it means," I said.

Marty glared at me. "I do. It means zip."

Carmen nodded. "I agree."

"I don't know what Dad's up to," Marty said. "But he'd never do anything to hurt Uncle Gene." He slid behind the steering wheel and snapped on his seatbelt.

Carmen gave me a dirty look. "I totally agree."

"Hey," I said, "I didn't say he did."

"And you better not," Marty said. "I don't care what your stupid lie detector tells you." He started the motor before I could answer.

When we got to Marty's, I said I was sorry, even though I hadn't really done anything.

Marty grinned and gave me a shove. "Don't get crazy on me, okay?"

"Listen," Carmen said, "I think we'd better go back out there tomorrow morning. Early."

"Good," I said. "Marty and I were supposed to go fishing anyway."

We all looked at each other for a second. Then Marty said, "He'll be all right tonight. He said he wouldn't sleep in the trailer."

Thirteen

On Saturday morning I woke up to the smell of blueberry muffins and the sound of Dave Brubeck's piano. When I staggered into the kitchen, Dad was already eating. "I didn't think you'd be up this early," he said.

I went to the refrigerator and got the milk. "I was having a dream when I heard a muffin call my name."

"These are spectacular muffins," Dad said. "Mrs. Lopez gave me the recipe."

I buttered a muffin, took a bite, and sighed. "They're better than spectacular," I whispered.

"I know," Dad said. "But I didn't want to brag."

I reached for another muffin. "If Mrs. Lopez ever offers you another recipe, take it."

Dad drank coffee and watched me plow through the plate of muffins. When I finally pushed back from the table, he said, "Now what? Are you going back to bed?"

"I'm going fishing with Marty today," I said. I'm not sure why I didn't mention Carmen.

"Where?" Dad asked.

"Ricketts Lake, I guess."

Dad leaned toward me. "Make it Ricketts Lake for sure. Nowhere else. And whatever you do, don't go near Uncle Gene's place."

"Why not?"

He got up from the table. "There's something wrong out there. Really wrong."

I didn't argue. At least Dad wasn't saying the fire was an accident.

Except for the creel, my fishing gear was still at Marty's. I strapped on the creel and rode my bike over to Carmen's. For once, I didn't even stop at the store for root beer.

Carmen must have been watching for me. By the time I stopped in front of her house, she was out the door.

"Ready to go?" I called before I got a good look at her.

She marched over to me. Her jaw was clamped shut and her eyes were full of fire. I didn't say a word. I just hoped that it wasn't me she was ready to kill.

"I can't go," she said, still clenching her jaw.

"What's the matter?"

"Mom says she has things for me to do," Carmen said. "But it's the same old stupid business. Girls aren't supposed to go running around the hills."

"Maybe it's not that," I told her. "My dad told me not to go near Uncle Gene's place. He knows something's wrong out there."

"So do my parents, even if they won't admit it. They almost died when they found out we'd gone out there yesterday afternoon."

I looked toward the house and saw Carmen's mother by the window. I wondered how much she'd heard. "I guess you miss the fishing trip then," I said, louder than before. "You want me to bring you back some trout?"

"No way," Carmen said. "If I catch one myself, I'll gag it down. Otherwise, forget it." She turned her back on the house and lowered her voice. "Stop by on your way back."

Marty had been given the same order I had—Ricketts Lake and nowhere else. "Mom didn't want me to take the buggy at all," he said.

"I don't get it," I said. "If they're all sure something's going to happen, why don't they try to stop it?"

"Mom tried," Marty said. "She went into town last night and called the sheriff."

I shrugged. "Maybe they'll believe her."

We put our poles and tackle boxes in the buggy and headed out the ridge trail. The buggy seat seemed awfully big now that I had it to myself. Marty drove right to the drop-off point for Ricketts Lake, then killed the motor. He unsnapped his seatbelt and stepped out. "You remember the good old days when we lived in a boring town? Right now SOT and MOTSOT don't sound so bad."

I climbed out of the buggy. "I just hope we don't come back and find the tires flat again."

We gathered up our fishing tackle, then looked at each other. "Do you really feel like fishing?" he asked.

"Get real."

"There's no way to do right," Marty said. "I want to make sure Uncle Gene's okay, and I got strict orders not to."

"Let's go," I said, climbing back into the buggy seat. "If we get in trouble, that's the breaks."

Marty held up his hand. "We don't want to get in trouble. If we do, we might not be able to come back out here at all."

"So what do we do?" I asked.

"We leave the buggy here," Marty said. "Dad's out gathering stuff today. He's likely to come by here just to check."

"You mean we walk the rest of the way?"

"You need the exercise anyway," he said. "You're getting a little flabby around the middle."

We stashed our fishing gear under a log and headed out the ridge trail. We started walking faster and faster, then ended up jogging on all but the steepest uphill stretches. It still took us a long time to get there.

We didn't yell until we could see down into the clearing and make sure nobody was parked there. I didn't want some guy telling Dad he'd seen me out at Gene's.

Uncle Gene didn't answer, but we didn't expect him to. When we came past the corral, the sheep ran toward us and stuck their heads through the rails, bleating away.

"They act hungry," Marty said.

"Watch out for Leonard," I said, trotting away from the fence. "He's got his ears back."

While we headed for the trailer, I looked over at the ashes of the cabin. It was weird looking at those gray piles and trying to remember exactly what the place had looked like. For some reason, I found myself thinking about my mother.

We kept yelling for Uncle Gene. I went up the trailer steps and tried the knob. It turned, and the door swung open. "Hey, Uncle Gene." I waited a second, then stepped inside.

A frying pan was sitting on the table. In the pan was one whole egg, sunny side up, and part of another, with a fork sticking in it. Next to the pan was a mug of coffee, almost full.

Marty came up the steps and looked in. "You figure he heard us coming and took off?"

"I guess." Stepping forward, I felt grit crunching under my shoe. I looked down and saw the pot of cactus, broken into pieces. The dirt from the pot had scattered in all directions.

"He must have gone outa here in a hurry," Marty said. "I guess we really spooked him."

I glanced at the eggs in the frying pan. The grease in the pan was solid and cold. "It wasn't us that spooked him," I said. "These eggs have been here awhile."

Just then I saw something brown on the bench. Even before I reached for it, I knew what it was—half a blueberry muffin. The same kind of spectacular muffins I'd had that morning.

So Dad had already been here.

"What is it?" Marty asked.

"Muffin," I said. "You hungry?" I wasn't ready to explain right then.

"I don't like this," Marty said, backing out the door. "Something's wrong here. We'd better go get some help."

"Let's take a quick look around first," I said. "Just to be sure Uncle Gene's not here."

"All right," Marty said. "But let's not mess around. This doesn't feel right at all."

"Check down by the creek," I said. "I'll go up by the water tank." I trotted over to the outhouse to make sure it was empty, then headed up to the water tank. When I got there, I stopped and yelled for Uncle Gene. The only sounds I heard were Marty shouting and the sheep bleating.

I made a circle through the trees. I didn't yell anymore. If Uncle Gene was around, he would have heard us by then. But he might have taken a fall or had a heart attack or something.

I ran past the mine shaft, then stopped. I suddenly had a feeling about that place. I didn't know anything for sure—it wasn't like one of the surges. But I wanted to check in there.

I bent down and took a few steps inside. By then I couldn't see a thing. I backed out into the light. Marty was still calling and the sheep were bleating their heads off.

I ran back to the trailer, rushed inside, and started yanking open drawers. I would have liked a flashlight or even a candle, but I settled for a book of matches that was sitting by the stove. I was halfway back to the mine before I thought about getting some paper to make a torch. But I didn't go back.

I crept into the shaft, running my hands along the sides to guide myself. When I'd gone as far as I could stand, I struck a match. At first I couldn't see anything but the flame. But when I held it in front of me, I could see the open shaft a few feet ahead. I rushed forward, wanting to make full use of the light. I only stopped when the match burned my fingers. I dropped it and the flame died.

I glanced back over my shoulder. The shaft opening looked tiny.

Then I heard a thud. And another. And another. The noises were coming from deeper in the shaft.

My first thought was of a cave-in, and I took a couple of quick steps backward. But what I heard didn't sound like a cave-in—whatever a cave-in sounded like. These were hollow pounding sounds, like somebody using a pick maybe.

I struck another match and hurried forward. The match blew out right away. I listened to the pounding for a few seconds, then crept forward a few steps before striking another match.

That time I cupped my hand to protect the flame and walked forward, banging my head once when I didn't duck far enough. The pounding got louder. Just before my match went out, I spotted something up ahead.

I tore off another match but paused before I lit it. I thought about running back to get Marty. It was stupid not to have brought him in the first place. But I'd come too far by then. I lit another match.

The first thing that I recognized was a boot, banging up and down on the floor of the shaft. A second later, I saw eyes reflecting the light of the match. Then I saw the beard. "Uncle Gene," I said.

I lit another match. Uncle Gene was sitting on the ground, his back against a wooden support post. His legs, not pounding now, were pointed toward me. I moved up close. "Are you all right?"

He made a grunting sound, and I saw the handkerchief tied over his mouth. I stepped between his feet before my match flickered out.

I used one more match to locate the knot. Then I worked in the dark, using my fingertips to pull at the loose ends. When the handkerchief came loose, Uncle Gene took three or four long breaths. "Bless you, boy," he muttered, then sucked in more air.

I lit another match so that I could get at his hands, which

were held together behind the post. But his hands weren't tied. He had a pair of silver handcuffs on his wrists. "I can't get you loose," I said. "I'll have to get a hacksaw."

"Run for it," Uncle Gene whispered. "The guy's still around here."

"Who?" I asked.

"I don't know. But he's after my papers. He's out there right now lookin' for 'em. You get outa here. Get some help."

"But what about—" I began.

"I'll be all right," Uncle Gene said. "He wants those papers, and I'm the only one who knows where they are. So he's gotta take care of me. Now get goin'."

I turned and headed for the opening. With that circle of daylight to aim for, I ducked my head and ran. I stopped a few feet from the opening and listened. When I didn't hear anything, I dashed out into the light and kept running until I was in the trees.

I circled back by the water tank, hoping to spot Marty. He wasn't yelling anymore.

The guy who had put Uncle Gene in the mine shaft couldn't be too far away. Marty and I had made plenty of noise to warn him that we were coming. He could easily have moved into the brush and waited. I looked around quickly, realizing that he could be watching me right at that moment.

I had to get help. But I hated to leave Marty behind. Staying in the trees, I hurried around behind the outhouse. I stopped now and then to look out into the clearing. The only movements I saw were the sheep and Leonard moving around the corral.

I didn't want to cross the open ground by the corral, so I

made a loop uphill. Once the corral and trailer were out of sight, I dashed across the road, staying in the trees while I headed for the creek.

I was almost there when I heard a yell, a deep-voiced shout: "Hey!" Then there was a clanging sound, metal on metal.

I dropped to my knees and crawled through the scrub oaks to the creek side of the corral. I stopped a foot short of the corral fence. The sheep came running toward me and stuck their heads through the rails. "Go on," I whispered, which didn't help at all.

The clanging started again. I dropped to my stomach and tried to see around the sheep's legs. A man with a hood over his head was standing next to the trailer. With his left hand, he was banging a shovel against the trailer. In his right hand was a black pistol. "Hey!" he yelled.

Lying on the ground, close to the man's feet, was Marty. His back was bare. His sweatshirt was wrapped around his head.

Again the man banged the trailer with the shovel. "Hey!"

Too many things had happened too fast, and I was having trouble keeping up. I'd been lying there for a minute or two before I figured out what the man was doing. He thought I was still up the hill. He was staying out of sight and calling me. He wanted me to hear the noise and come running.

For the moment he had his back to me. If he turned around and saw the sheep breaking down the fence, I'd be finished. I scooted backward into the brush. Leonard stuck his head over the top rail and spit in my direction.

I was almost to the creek when I realized that I hadn't

really looked at the man. All I'd seen was the hood. I stopped and crept back for a quick last look. It didn't help. From that distance, all I could see was somebody wearing a denim jacket and jeans. He tossed the shovel aside and walked away from the trailer, his body swinging with each step.

I dropped to my stomach and slid backward until I was behind the scrub oaks. Then I got up and crept across the creek and worked my way uphill, keeping away from any open spots. When I hit the ridge road, I was already moving at a dead run.

Fourteen

While I raced down the ridge road, I kept thinking about the man with the hood. If he was someone I knew, I should have been able to recognize something about him. But I came up empty. He was just a man.

I thought about the blueberry muffin I'd seen in the trailer and asked myself the obvious question: Could the man in the hood be Dad? And I had to admit that he could. But he could have been Mr. McNabb too. Or Amos Lawlor. Or anybody else in town.

And once I thought about it, I wasn't even sure it was a man. It might have been Mrs. Lopez. Except that she was too short. Maybe.

So there I was running for help, and maybe running right straight for the person who caused the trouble. Except that that person wouldn't be home. That was the only good news.

I ran all the way to the brush buggy, gritting my teeth and trying to ignore the sideaches and the stomach cramps. By the time I got there, my head was reeling, and black dots were flashing across my eyes. I slid in behind the steering wheel, but my hands were shaking so much that I had trouble holding on to the key long enough to start the engine.

I'd only driven the buggy a few times, and the clutch always gave me trouble. I killed the motor twice before I got the buggy backed around and headed down the ridge. Once I had it going in the right direction, though, I held the wheel tightly and shoved the gas pedal to the floor.

Even then, the buggy just crept along. I could have run almost as fast. On the downhill stretches, when I should have been barreling along, the gearing held me to a crawl.

I finally figured out a system. I'd drive with the engine wide open up the hills and over the top. Then when I hit the steep downhill runs, I shoved in the clutch. That way, nothing held me back.

I should have known better. In fact, I did know better. But I kept thinking of Marty lying on the ground with his sweatshirt over his head. I told myself that in a few minutes I'd have the buggy back at Marty's place, and I'd never drive like that again.

But I pushed too hard. The buggy came tearing down a long hill and couldn't make the turn at the bottom. The right front tire started up the bank. I yanked the steering wheel the other way, and the buggy began to spin. I jammed on the brake. Trees and brush flashed past. Clouds of dirt poured over me, blocking out everything else. The buggy smacked something, throwing me sideways, but I still kept spinning.

Through the dust, I watched a tree slide slowly past me before the buggy ground to a stop. I sat for a second, my hands still locked on the wheel. My mouth was full of dirt.

The only sound was my own heavy breathing, and I realized that the motor had died.

I checked the buggy. The tires still had air and the frame looked the same. So I shoved in on the clutch and twisted the key. Nothing happened. I twisted the key once more, then unsnapped my seatbelt and hit the ground running.

While I ran, I had to decide whether to head for the McNabbs' or for town. The McNabbs' place was a little closer, but if nobody was home there, I'd have a bike ride ahead of me. The thought of climbing onto my bicycle was enough to send me toward town.

I just kept running. My throat was raw, and my mouth was filled with a rusty-nails taste. I fell twice, for no reason. I just went tumbling face first into the dirt. Both times I scrambled up without ever stopping.

I didn't think about anything. The words of "The Happy Wanderer" kept bouncing around inside my head. Then, later, my feet were pounding the ground in rhythm with "Row, Row, Row Your Boat."

When I came over a rise and got my first glimpse of the town down below, I tried to yell "Fire." If I could get somebody to ring the fire bell, people would be at the store, ready for action, by the time I got there. But I couldn't manage anything but a croak, even when I stopped running for a second.

I raced down the last long slope. Whenever I came to an open spot, I waved my hand over my head. If people saw me running and waving, they might get the idea that something was wrong. But I knew my chances were bad. Nobody in town ever looked up at the mountain.

When the ridge road gets close to town, it splits into a dozen trails, each one running down to a driveway or somebody's pasture. Without thinking about it, I took the trail that passes the old barn and comes out by Carmen's place.

I spotted Carmen out in their garden, watering the flowers. I managed to squeeze out a yell, something like "Hey-uh." She turned in my direction, dropped the hose, and came running up the road.

The weird look on her face scared me. It was that wide-eyed look you see in the movies when people are running from Godzilla. I figured I must look almost as bad as I felt.

"What happened?" she shouted.

Panting the way I was, I could only get out one word with each breath. "Ring . . . the . . . fire . . . bell."

For once, Carmen didn't ask any questions. She spun around, dashed back to their garage, grabbed her bicycle, and took off down the road. By the time I staggered into her yard, I heard the bell clanging.

I stumbled over and grabbed the hose she had dropped. I sucked in water for a long time, then raised the hose above my head. Water poured over my hair and down my back while I caught my breath. Then I drank some more.

I was still under the hose when Carmen came riding back. She skidded to a stop, laid her bike on the ground, and ran to me. She took the hose from me and used her hand to bathe my face. "Are you all right?" she asked, running her fingers through my wet hair.

"I guess." My breath was coming a little easier.

"You've got to get up to the store. You want to ride my bike?"

I grabbed the hose from her and took one more drink. "I can't."

She ran over and lifted up the bike. "Sit sideways on the crossbar. I'll pump."

We went wobbling up the road. Men in pickups roared past us.

Ten or twelve people were in front of the store, and more trucks and cars were pulling into the parking lot. Carmen stopped beside the porch, and I slid off the bar. Dad jumped out of his truck and came running over to us.

"Carmen rang the bell," Mrs. Lopez was yelling. "She's the one."

"What happened?" Dad asked me. People around us were staring and shaking their heads.

"Did he get hit by a car?" one woman asked.

"How'd he get so wet?" somebody else asked.

"Uncle Gene," I told Dad. "A guy's got him tied up in the mine. And he's got Marty too."

Dad's eyes narrowed. "Does he have a gun?"

I nodded. "Yeah."

"All right," Dad called to the crowd. "There's trouble at Uncle Gene's. Somebody's out there with a gun."

People ran for their trucks. Some of the men yelled about getting their rifles. "I'll call the sheriff," Mrs. Lopez said.

Carmen's mother came marching across the porch. "Carmen," she called out, "don't even think about it."

"But, Mom—" Carmen moaned.

Her mother pointed a finger. "I mean it."

"It's not fair," Carmen said. She ran with me to Dad's pickup. For a second I thought she was going to climb in.

Then she stepped aside and said, "I hate this so bad."

Two minutes later I was bouncing along in Dad's pickup, wedged between him and Mr. Lopez. We were third in a line of seven trucks. Dust was flying in all directions. "Did you run all the way from Uncle Gene's?" Dad asked me.

"Just about."

"That's a long, long ways," Mr. Lopez muttered. He had his right hand resting on the roof of the truck to hold himself in place.

Dad looked over at me. "When you've got your breath back, I want to hear all about it."

I told him what we'd done. When I tried to talk about Marty with the sweatshirt over his head, my hands started shaking and tears ran down my face.

Mr. Lopez smiled and elbowed me in the ribs. "This is some kind of kid."

"So you're pretty sure there's just one man?" Dad asked.

"Yeah."

"What do you think he's doing?" Mr. Lopez asked. I wasn't sure whether he was talking to Dad or me. Neither of us answered him.

"He's bound to be gone by this time," Dad said.

"He better be," Mr. Lopez said.

Dad didn't say anything more for a while, but I knew it was coming. I felt him take several long breaths and let them out slowly. Then he said, "I told you not to go there, and you went."

I didn't have any answer for that. I just hoped Marty was all right.

Fifteen

Half a mile from Uncle Gene's, the trucks ahead of us braked to a stop. Guido Cavalo came trotting back toward us. "Think we ought to walk in from here?" he asked Dad.

"There was just one man," Dad said. "He's long gone by now."

"No telling what a guy like that might do," Guido said. "I don't mind going first, but it might be smart to move in slow."

When he said that, I felt a surge run up my arms.

"I'll go ahead," Dad told him. He pulled out of line and eased the pickup past the others.

"You're going first?" Mr. Lopez asked.

"The guy's gone by now," Dad told him.

Mr. Lopez let out a low whistle.

"You want to ride with somebody else?" Dad asked him.

Mr. Lopez didn't answer for a second. Then he grinned. "Let's go. But you better be right. If I get shot, my wife'll kill me."

Dad guided the pickup around the worst of the ruts. I glanced back and saw that the others were coming, but they weren't crowding us.

"You might as well get down, Sam," Dad said. "Just in case."

"No use taking a chance," Mr. Lopez said. He slid down in the seat until his head was below the window.

I ducked down for a minute, then raised my head enough so that I could look through the windshield. I guess I was scared. But I was too tired to feel much.

Dad drove up to the trailer and climbed out, with me right behind him. I heard a banging noise, and the trailer rocked a little. I ran to the other side where the steps were.

"Wait a minute," Dad shouted.

But I was already on the steps. I pushed open the door. It banged into something, and I heard a grunt. Marty was lying there on the floor.

"It's okay," I said. I unfastened the belt around his head and pulled the sweatshirt off his face. He took a deep breath and blew it out. "Oh, baby, I was suffocating."

Dad stuck his head in the door. "Are you all right, Marty?"

"Better than I was," Marty said.

Dad took out his pocketknife and sliced through the shoe-lace tied around Marty's wrists.

"Do I still have hands?" Marty asked. "I can't feel them at all."

Dad reached down and untied Marty's ankles. "You'll feel them in a minute."

"I thought you'd never get back," Marty said to me.

That was a rotten thing to say to somebody who'd run the

way I had, but I figured time went slow when you had a sweatshirt over your head.

By then, most of the men were standing around. "Uncle Gene's in the mine shaft," Dad said.

"Where's that?" somebody asked.

"Up this way," Mr. Lopez said. The men followed him.

"Get a hacksaw," I called. "He's handcuffed to a post."

Marty started flapping his hands and banging them against his legs. "Ay-yi-yi!" he said. "It's like bee stings."

"Who did this to you?" Dad asked him.

Marty kept flapping his hands. "I don't know. It's so stupid, but I don't have the foggiest idea."

"How'd it happen?" I asked.

"I was waiting for you," Marty said. "The sheep were going crazy, so I thought I'd get some hay for them. The guy was inside the shed. He grabbed me from behind, put a pistol to my head, and shoved my face in the hay. Then he pulled my sweatshirt up over my head, and I couldn't see a thing."

"Did he say anything?" I asked.

"Not much—just go, sit. Stuff like that. But he talked funny. His voice was real deep, and he pronounced the words funny: 'Seet' and 'Wass you name?' Like that."

"Foreigner?" Dad asked.

"Maybe," Marty said. "Or maybe he was disguising his voice."

"We're not much help," I said. "He had a hood over his head when I saw him. He could have been anybody."

"The only thing I know," Marty said, "is he's got big feet. When he shoved me in here, I got a look at his boots. Size fourteen or so."

"That's something," Dad said. He looked around outside and located a couple of bootprints.

Once Dad was out of sight, Marty whispered, "Are you in trouble?"

"Probably," I said. "He was too worried to say much yet."

Marty came out and sat on the trailer steps. His face was white, and he was rocking back and forth. "Are you okay?" I asked him.

"Kinda dizzy."

I ran over and shoved his head down between his legs. His whole body was shaking. "Take it easy," I said. "Don't even talk."

After a minute he got a little color in his cheeks. He sat up slowly. "I just about lost it there."

"If you start feeling funny, put your head down again."

"Where'd you learn that?"

"I know all kinds of things," I said. Actually, somebody did that for me at my mother's funeral, but I didn't tell him that.

Uncle Gene was no more help than we were. The men sawed his handcuffs in two, then brought him back to the trailer with the rings still on his wrists. While the others were trying to figure the easiest way to cut off the rings, Uncle Gene marched up and down. "By golly, I showed him," he yelled. "Guy tried to scare me. But I don't scare easy."

It took a while to get the story, but, the way Uncle Gene told it, he was eating breakfast when something crashed into the trailer. "I was right in the middle of those muffins you brought me," he told Dad. Uncle Gene came running out the door to investigate. The guy grabbed him and slapped a blindfold on him. So Uncle Gene hadn't seen any more than Marty and I had.

Once Uncle Gene was blindfolded and handcuffed, the guy tried to make him tell where his papers were. But Uncle Gene wouldn't. Finally the guy took him up to the mine and left him there.

Later on, the guy came back and told Uncle Gene he had Marty. If Uncle Gene didn't hand over the papers, something bad would happen. "I wasn't about to let him hurt my buddy here," Uncle Gene said, grinning away. "So I told him the papers were in the woodshed at the school."

That got everybody's attention. "Why didn't you tell us before?" somebody yelled.

Uncle Gene held up his hand. "Lies. All of it. I said I was scared to leave my papers around here when I went to Elk Meadow. So I took 'em to town. Then I couldn't leave 'em sittin' in the Jeep, so I hid 'em in the woodshed."

Guido Cavalo laughed. "You old rascal."

Uncle Gene kept on grinning. "The guy swallowed it whole. Took off like a shot."

Some of the men were confused, and Uncle Gene went back and told the story over again. Meanwhile one of the men had found a piece of leather. They slid the leather underneath the metal ring around Uncle Gene's wrist. That way, they could use the hacksaw without sawing Uncle Gene. It was slow going, but the rest of the day was even slower.

Nobody wanted to leave until the sheriff came. Some of the men stretched out in the shade and took naps. And one guy dug out a rod and reel and went fishing in Uncle Gene's creek.

Dr. Vincent came driving up in his Range Rover. He parked by the trailer and took charge right away. "You need to do your statements while things are still fresh in your mind," he told us. He had Marty and me write down everything that had happened. He wanted Uncle Gene to do the same, but Uncle Gene said he'd wait for the sheriff. So Dr. Vincent got somebody else to write down the story while Uncle Gene told it.

When Dr. Vincent looked over my shoulder to read what I was writing, I caught a whiff of something nasty. I recognized the stink but couldn't think what it was. I glanced down at his boots to see if he'd stepped in something. But that wasn't it.

He didn't like my report. "You need to put in the times, son. Be specific."

"I wasn't looking at my watch," I said.

"Estimate," he said. "Work backward. Calculate how long each thing took." He figured that if we could pin down the times, we'd give the sheriff a head start.

Dad said he'd left Uncle Gene's place about eight o'clock. Marty and I had no idea when we'd gotten there, but we said nine so that Dr. Vincent would leave us alone.

The only excitement came when Mr. NcNabb showed up. He skidded to a stop by the corral, jumped out of his truck, and yelled, "Is Marty here?" Somebody pointed him toward the trailer, and he came running.

When Marty stepped out, Mr. McNabb stopped and said, "Are you all right?"

"I'm fine," Marty said.

Mr. McNabb walked toward the trailer with those long steps of his. "I don't know whether to hug you or hit you." He grabbed Marty and wrapped his arms around him. "You scared the fool outa me. I came home, and Carmen said you'd been kidnapped."

Marty told him what had happened. He got a little shaky while he talked. I thought he might have to get his head between his legs again. Mr. McNabb moved from one foot to the other. He looked like he *still* wasn't sure whether to hit Marty or hug him.

"We're outa here," Mr. McNabb said when Marty finished. "I want to get back before your mother comes home and hears the news."

"He'd better stay here," Dr. Vincent said. "The sheriff will want to talk to him."

"Tell him where we live," Mr. McNabb said.

"He won't like it," Dr. Vincent said.

Mr. McNabb shrugged. "That's too bad. But I'm a lot more scared of my wife than I am of the sheriff." That got some people laughing.

"Be sure and leave your statement," Dr. Vincent told Marty.

Deputy Bates showed up about two o'clock. Dr. Vincent rushed over and started explaining things. Bates nodded and said, "Uh-huh." That's also what he did when they showed him the sawed-through handcuffs. And what he did when he looked at the footprints and our statements.

People started to leave. They were hungry by then, and watching Bates nod his head and grunt got old in a hurry. "The way he's going at it," Mr. Lopez said, "the crook'll die of old age before they catch him."

After Bates had seen everything, he sat in his car for a long time, writing in a notebook. By then, only a handful of us were left.

Bates climbed out of the car and waved his hand. "Uncle Gene, let's go to town."

"I got things to do," Uncle Gene said.

"You're going to town first," Bates told him.

Uncle Gene fussed, but it didn't help. Bates planned to telephone the sheriff from Alder Creek, and he wanted Uncle Gene there in case the sheriff had a question.

"I'll come," Uncle Gene said finally. "But I'll come with these two." He put his arms around Dad and me. "You guys go ahead, and we'll be right behind."

We got into the pickup and let the others start out. "Hold it a second," Uncle Gene said. He stepped out and hurried up the hill toward the outhouse. Dad backed the pickup over that way.

When Uncle Gene came away from the outhouse, he had a knapsack in his hand. He pulled open the pickup door and climbed in beside me. "Nobody'd ever think of looking there," he said. "I put it under the floorboards. Safer than any bank." He let out a laugh.

I couldn't keep my eyes off that ratty knapsack. It was hard to believe that there was something inside it that had caused a man to burn down a house and kidnap people.

Uncle Gene saw me looking at it. "Them papers are worth money," he said. "Big money."

Sixteen

Dad drove right past the store, calling out, "We'll be right there," to the people on the porch. At our house, Dad slapped together roast beef sandwiches for us. Uncle Gene came inside, stripped off his shirt, and put on the knapsack. When he put on his shirt again, the knapsack made a big hump between his shoulder blades. I didn't see the point.

We drove back to the store, and everybody came off the porch to see Uncle Gene. In no time he was sitting on a bench, telling his story again.

I told Carmen everything, finishing with, "So you didn't miss much by not going out there."

She glared at me. "That's not the point. It's just so stupid— because I'm a girl, I'm supposed to sit home and wait."

Deputy Bates came over and handed me my statement. "Think, boy. About how tall was this guy?"

"Kind of tall, I guess."

Bates waved his hand toward the people on the porch.

"Look at these people. Was he bigger than him? Or him? What about our friend Mr. Lawlor there? Bigger or smaller?" Amos Lawlor sneered at us and turned away.

"I'm not sure."

Then Bates pointed at Dad. "Was he taller than your dad or shorter?"

I looked at Dad. "About the same, I guess." Then I realized how that sounded.

But Bates just nodded and said, "Uh-huh." He looked at the paper. "You said the guy walked funny. Like how?"

"It's hard to explain."

"Show us," Carmen said.

I moved into the open and tried to walk the way the guy had, throwing my body around with each step.

"You look like your feet hurt," Carmen said.

"Maybe that's it," I said, trotting back to them. "Maybe those big boots didn't really fit him."

"Uh-huh," Bates said. I couldn't tell if he'd thought of that before or not.

Marty and his parents showed up after that. Bates had sent Dr. Vincent to get them. Bates took Marty over to the patrol car and talked to him.

When Mrs. Lopez called Bates to the telephone, Marty wandered over to where Carmen and I were standing. "Did you confess?" I asked him.

Marty grinned. "I feel so stupid. You know how much help I was? Zip. Zilch. Zero. The only thing I saw were those big boots, and Bates thinks they were part of the disguise."

"Well," Carmen said, "at least Mom will quit saying the fire was an accident."

Deputy Bates came back outside. "Uncle Gene," he said, "the sheriff wants to talk to you."

Uncle Gene got up and started for the door.

"Not on the phone," Bates said. "He wants you to come to Yreka."

Uncle Gene sat down again. "If he wants to talk, he can come see me. And he can bring along the hundred dollars he owes me."

"Come on," Bates said. "It's a good day for a ride."

Uncle Gene pushed himself up from the bench. "I'd better go to the bathroom first."

Bates nodded and said, "Uh-huh."

People stepped aside, and Uncle Gene headed into the store. "I need some coffee," he said to Bates. "You gonna buy me a cup?" He went down the aisle toward the back door and the rest rooms.

"I'll spring for the coffee," Bates said, stepping inside the store. "I might have a cup myself." He brought his cup out onto the porch, stirring it with a wooden stick.

Two or three minutes went by. Carmen and I looked at each other. "I don't think anybody's gonna drink that other coffee," Marty muttered.

Bates finished his coffee and stepped back inside. "Could I get a refill?" he said. Then he headed toward the rest rooms. He was back in less than a minute. "The old guy ran off."

"We can find him," Dr. Vincent called out. "Come on, men. He can't be very far. Let's spread out and look for him."

About half the men went with Dr. Vincent, but most of them were smiling. Everybody knew it was a waste of time. Nobody was going to catch Uncle Gene.

I watched a rented video that night, but I kept falling asleep, then backing up the tape. Finally, when I woke up and saw a man I didn't recognize kissing a woman I didn't recognize, I flipped off the machine and headed for bed.

As soon as I turned on my bedroom light, I heard a tapping sound. The first thing I thought of was the guy in the hood. I backed against the wall and looked around me.

The tapping came again. Somebody was outside my window. I crept over there.

A face pressed up against the glass—nose flattened, eyes flashing, hair everywhere. I yelped and jumped back. Then I saw the white beard and recognized Uncle Gene.

I hurried over and raised the window. My heart was doing about two hundred beats a minute. "Uncle Gene," I said. "What's going on?"

He grinned at me. "I'm too old to sleep on the ground without no blankets or nothing," he said. "You think you could help me out?"

"Sure." I moved back from the window. "You want to climb in here?"

"I'm too old to be climbing in windows too."

"Come around to the front door," I said.

I walked back to the living room and held the door open. He stood in the dark of the porch and looked around, then hurried inside. He was still wearing the knapsack underneath his shirt. I closed the door and bolted it.

"I couldn't go back to my place," he whispered. "That guy might be out there waiting for me. And he's prob'ly plenty mad about how I fooled him today."

"You'll be fine here." I started back to my bedroom.

Uncle Gene stayed where he was. "You know that roast beef your dad had? Real nice and tender. You suppose he's got any left?"

So I made him a huge sandwich that he polished off in no time. "How about another one for dessert?" I asked. I expected him to laugh, but he didn't see any joke in it.

"If it's not too much trouble, boy."

When he'd finished his second sandwich, we went down the hall to my bedroom. I stood on my desk chair and hauled a sleeping bag and blanket out of the cupboard above my closet. I spread the blanket on the floor and put the sleeping bag on top. "You can have my bed," I told him.

"Not a chance, boy. This is perfect. I like it a little hard." He pulled off his boots and slid into the sleeping bag. Then he took off his shirt and the knapsack. He wrapped the shirt around the knapsack and used the whole bundle for a pillow.

"I can get you a regular pillow," I said.

"I like it this way, boy. I don't need nothing fancy. I just can't take the cold like I used to."

He was asleep and snoring in no time—a grunting, whining snore. Figuring I'd never be able to sleep with that racket going, I decided to try the couch in the living room. But I drifted off before I got up the energy to make the move.

In the morning Dad woke us for breakfast. "Glad you stopped by, Uncle Gene," he said. "I was hoping you wouldn't go back out to your place."

"I didn't want no more surprises," Uncle Gene said, pulling on his shirt.

After a breakfast of apple pancakes, Dad offered to drive Uncle Gene out to his place. "You gotta feed Leonard and the sheep sometime," Dad said.

"You got a gun around here?" Uncle Gene asked.

"Sure," Dad said.

Uncle Gene shrugged. "Then I guess we can go. I'll get my boots."

The only gun we had was a single-shot .22 rifle. We didn't have any shells, but Dad got it out just the same.

Uncle Gene was in my bedroom a long time. I thought maybe he'd gone out the window, so I walked over to the door to check. But I could hear him clumping around in there.

When he finally came out, he said, "I put away your bedroll. I didn't want to leave no mess."

He was wearing his knapsack under his shirt again. "You might be more comfortable if you kept that thing in your lap," Dad told him.

"I'm not complaining."

We didn't argue with him. Dad put the empty rifle behind the seat of the pickup, and we drove off.

The only trouble we had was with Leonard, who was in a spitting mood, probably mad about getting a late breakfast. Dad and I stayed out of the way while Uncle Gene forked some hay out of the shed.

"I might as well stay here," Uncle Gene said afterward. "Can't make no money in town."

But Dad didn't have much trouble talking him into coming back with us.

When we drove past the store, I saw the sheriff's car sitting there. It pulled out right away and followed us to our place.

Before we could get out of the truck, Deputy Bates was right beside Uncle Gene's door. "You're coming with me, Uncle Gene."

"Where?"

Bates pulled open the door. "Yreka."

Uncle Gene shook his head. "Nothing in Yreka I want."

"Did you like wearing those handcuffs yesterday?" Bates asked him. "I got another pair right here. It's up to you. You can cooperate or not, but you're coming with me either way."

Uncle Gene looked over at Dad and me. "Well, boys, I believe I'll go to Yreka. I want to see the sheriff about the hundred bucks he owes me."

When the patrol car drove off, I started thinking about Deputy Bates being in exactly the right place at the right time. "Dad," I said, "don't you think that was a little funny? It was almost like Deputy Bates knew we were coming."

Dad started for the house. "Maybe he was just lucky."

A surge ran up my arm, but I would have known anyway. "Dad," I said, "you phoned him, didn't you?"

He turned back and looked at me. "Yeah. I didn't want anything to happen to the old guy. At least he'll be safe for a couple of days."

I was disgusted. "You could have told me," I said.

He smiled. "Best way to keep a secret is not to tell anybody."

He had a point, I guess. But I didn't like it.

I planned to walk over to Marty's and get my bike, but Dad drove me there. "No use taking chances," he said.

The brush buggy was sitting in the yard. A rooster was

asleep on the driver's seat. Marty and Mr. McNabb had gotten the buggy the night before. "Took us about thirty seconds to get it started," Marty told me. "One of the battery cables had come loose." He showed me the cable so that I'd know next time. But I figured there wouldn't be a next time.

While Mr. McNabb showed Dad their vegetable garden, I told Marty about Uncle Gene spending the night. "That's good," Marty said. "After we got the buggy going, Dad and I drove out there. We were gonna have him come home with us."

"Now what?" I said. "They can't keep Uncle Gene in Yreka forever."

"I hope they catch this guy soon," Marty said. "I can't use the brush buggy."

"Don't feel bad. Dad wouldn't even let me walk over here."

Marty leaned against the back tire of the buggy. "You think Deputy Bates will come up with anything?"

I shook my head. "He doesn't know anything we don't. And we don't know beans."

"I oughta know more than I do," Marty said. "The guy tied me up, and I heard him talk. I shoulda noticed something."

"At least you have an excuse," I said. "Your eyes were covered up. I actually saw the guy. And he could have been anybody at all." I glanced over at the garden where Mr. McNabb was kneeling by a tomato plant. "For all I know, it could have been my dad or your dad." I had wanted to ease into the subject, but that just popped out.

Marty pushed me, a little harder than usual. "Don't start that crazy stuff."

"Okay," I said, backing away from him. "To us, it's crazy. But look at it the way Bates would. It had to be somebody who knows the area. Now forget they're our fathers for a second—"

"No," Marty cut in, "I don't want to forget, and you shouldn't either."

"Come on. I'm just talking."

"You're getting weird again." He turned away from me and started fiddling with the buggy's fanbelt.

When Dad and Mr. McNabb came out of the garden, they were talking about Uncle Gene. They didn't have any answers either.

"The people in town say old Gene has a silent partner," Mr. McNabb said. "Maybe somebody smells money."

"I don't know if Uncle Gene's got a partner," Dad said, "but anybody that smells money around him better get his nose fixed."

I wasn't really listening. I was watching Marty adjust the fanbelt. But while Dad was talking, I felt the old surge run up my arms. Marty was right—it was crazy. But the surge was there all the same. Dad was lying again.

I felt as lonely as I'd ever felt. I wanted to tell somebody—just pour out the whole thing. Then I wanted somebody to explain where I'd gone wrong. I had to be wrong somewhere.

Dad could have done it all—I knew that. He could have taken the muffins out to Uncle Gene, then left his truck and come back in disguise. He could have done all the things Uncle Gene said and still beat me to town.

But Dad wouldn't do anything like that.

Besides, what could he get out of it? Even if Uncle Gene

had hit a bonanza, which I didn't believe for a minute, so what? Dad didn't care that much about money. And what other reason could he have?

But he'd lied. Over and over.

I felt lost—and alone. I couldn't tell anybody. Not even Marty.

I was all alone—smack in the middle of nowhere.

I walked over and sat on a tire. I might need to put my head between my legs any second.

Seventeen

The rest of Sunday was MOTSOT, sitting around and trying to make sense of things. I took Saturday's video back to the store. I'd only seen half of it, but that was enough.

While I was standing by the video rack, Mr. and Mrs. Lawlor came in. She walked past me like she'd never seen me before. Not him. He stared me down, then muttered, "The big hero," when he walked past.

I grabbed a new video, paid for it, and ran all the way home. I didn't want to be on the road when the Lawlors drove by.

I ended up watching the video twice, and it was lousy the first time. Dad stayed in his room and read a book.

I felt rotten. How could I figure things out when there were so many things I didn't know? And the most confusing part of all was the one thing I was sure of—Dad was lying.

All night I thought about going into his room and talking to him. But I couldn't think of a way to start. So I just sat there like a slug.

After Dad left for work on Monday, I washed the breakfast dishes and got ready for school. When I reached into my closet for a shirt, I saw a green cord hanging down from the cupboard above. It was one of the cords from the sleeping bag Uncle Gene had used.

I stood on tiptoes to pry open the cupboard door, but I couldn't quite reach the sleeping bag to stuff in the cord. Too lazy to walk across the room and get my desk chair, I yanked on the cord and pulled down the bag. I tucked away the cord, then jumped up and stuffed the bag back into place. Two points.

But when the bag landed, I heard a crackling sound that wasn't right. I got my desk chair, climbed up, and pushed the bag to one side. The only thing under it was the blanket Uncle Gene had used. I pushed down on the blanket and heard the sound of crinkling papers.

I got my hands under the blanket, lifted it up, stepped off the chair, and set the blanket on my bed. Then I unfolded it carefully.

I've watched too many videos. I had a crazy idea that I was going to unfold the blanket and finds stacks of money—big wads of bills with wrappers around them.

But it wasn't money. It was just four dirty manila envelopes, all stuffed with papers. I undid the clasp of each envelope and peeked inside. Just the old photocopies and maps I'd seen a dozen times before.

I folded the blanket around the envelopes again and put it back in the cupboard with the sleeping bag on top. That seemed as good a hiding place as any, especially since everybody would figure the papers were in Yreka with Uncle Gene.

I rushed over to school. Billy Cavalo came running to meet me. "Mr. Harrison's back," he called back.

"Good," I said, looking around for Marty.

"I told him we didn't miss him one bit."

Marty and Carmen were standing by the monkey bars. I knew what they'd be talking about. But I had a little something to add to the conversation. I jogged over.

"It has to be somebody from town," Carmen was saying.

"Guess what I found this morning," I said.

"An early birthday present for me," Carmen said.

"What?" Marty asked.

"Uncle Gene's papers. He left them at our house."

"Really?" a voice said from behind me. I spun around. It was Billy Cavalo. He'd followed me clear across the schoolyard.

"I was just teasing," I said.

"I'll bet you weren't."

"Sure I was. I was just playing a joke on Carmen."

"He does that all the time," Carmen said.

Billy shook his head and backed away. "Huh-uh."

I gave up on that. "Come here, Billy." When he moved a little closer, Marty and I ran and grabbed him. I took his arms, Marty got his legs, and we swung him high in the air. "Don't drop him," I said. "Billy's our buddy."

"We wouldn't hurt Billy," Marty said.

"Listen, Billy," I said, "don't tell anybody what you heard, all right? If you do, you won't be our buddy anymore."

"I won't tell," Billy said.

"Make him cross his heart," Carmen said.

"Billy's no squealer," I said. We set him down on the ground, and I gave him a high five. "He's our pal."

"Swing me again," Billy said. "Higher."

We kept Billy with us until Mr. Harrison came out, walking on crutches, and rang the bell. "Here we go," Marty said. "Back to SOT and MOTSOT."

"I was hoping your mom would be here for the rest of the year," I told him.

"So was she," Marty said. "She had a lot of fun."

"Listen," I said, "do you think Billy's all right? Will he keep his mouth shut?"

"No," Carmen said.

Marty shook his head. "Not a chance."

"Great," I said. "Now the guy's gonna come after me."

"Hey," Carmen said, "that's not such a bad idea."

"Thanks a lot."

"I'm serious. Unless we do something, we may never find out who it is."

"So what do you want to do?" I said. "Have him burn down my house?"

"Right," Carmen said. "And if he kills you, be sure and leave us one of those dying messages they have in the mystery stories."

"This is no joke," I told her. "Ask Marty."

"But we could do things so nobody was in danger," Carmen said. "What if we spread the word that you found the papers and you're scared to keep them in your house?"

"That's true enough," I said.

"As soon as it's dark," she went on, "you come out of your house and take some papers—any old papers—to some hiding place. And Marty and I can watch and see who follows you and gets the papers."

I thought about it for a minute. "That just might work."

"I hope so," Marty said. "Everything's too weird right now."

"We won't do anything stupid," Carmen said. "We'll just stay out of the way and see who it is."

"It's a good thing you're honest," I told Carmen. "You'd be a dynamite crook."

Mr. Harrison stuck his head out the door. "Hurry it up!"

"One last thing," I said. "How do we spread the word?"

"Easy," Marty said. "Tell Billy and make him promise not to tell. Every kid in school will know it before the day's over."

Marty was wrong. Every kid knew it by noon.

The minute school was out, I raced home and locked myself in the house. Then I checked every window and pulled down the shades.

I tried to come up with a hiding place that nobody would ever think of. I thought about the freezer, but there wasn't enough room.

I ended up sliding the four envelopes under the refrigerator. The floor was filthy under there, but so were the envelopes.

It was a long afternoon. I got some paper bags and stuffed them with newspapers. Those would be my fake papers. Then I read magazines and made a salad for dinner. I even did some homework that wasn't due for a week.

When I heard Dad drive in, I unlocked the door. He came inside, took off his boots, and walked into the kitchen. "Somebody at the store said you had Uncle Gene's papers."

I knew he'd hear the story, so I had my answer set: "That's Billy Cavalo for you. He heard us talking about the papers, and he started spreading stories."

I liked that answer—not exactly straight, maybe, but no lies.

"So you don't have the papers?"

I wasn't ready for that one, but I managed to say, "No, I don't have 'em." That wasn't exactly a lie. I knew where they were—under the refrigerator—but I didn't actually have them. But I felt crummy just the same.

Right after we ate, Dad said we'd better drive out to Uncle Gene's to feed Leonard and the sheep. I said I had too much homework.

"It won't take long," he said.

"I have a lot of stuff to do."

Dad shook his head. "I don't like leaving you here by yourself. Not with that rumor going around about the papers."

"Nobody believes anything Billy says."

"All right," he said finally. "But keep the doors locked. And if somebody knocks, don't open the door. Just say you're sick." Before he left, he telephoned the Hinshaws, our next door neighbors, and told them to keep an eye out.

I was feeling a lot better. If Dad was worried about somebody coming after the papers, then he couldn't be the guy.

I locked the door right away. Then I got our .22 rifle and

spent a while digging through drawers, looking for a bullet. I didn't find one.

There was nothing to do but wait. At 8:30 I was going out the front door and down the road to the school. I'd put the papers into a box in the bus garage. By then, Marty and Carmen would be waiting in the woodshed next to the garage.

If Dad was back by then, I'd have to slip out my bedroom window. But I didn't think he could get back that soon.

At 8:05 the telephone rang. I figured it was probably Carmen. Maybe she couldn't get away from her house.

I ran over and grabbed the receiver. "Hello."

"Listen," a deep voice said. Only it sounded like "Leeson."

I managed to say, "Yeah?"

"I got the girl. You bring the papers this minute. Put the papers by the school mailbox and go back home. Don't touch the phone. Don't tell nobody."

"Okay!" I shouted into the phone. "I'll do it!"

"Hurry!" the voice said. "Hurry fast!"

Eighteen

I slammed down the phone and ran to the kitchen. I flopped onto the floor and dragged the envelopes from under the refrigerator. One of them had been shoved back farther than I could reach, and I had to use the broom to get it.

I had too many things to think about. Where would the guy have Carmen? Would he let her go after he got the papers? Where was Marty?

I grabbed up the envelopes and ran for the front door. If I could have kept running, I probably would have. But I had to stop to unlock the door. That was just enough time to get me thinking. If I gave him the papers, then what? How could I be sure he'd let Carmen go? But if I gave him the fake papers, he might do something terrible.

I've always heard about people running in circles. That's what I ended up doing. I got the fake papers, then shoved the real ones under the couch cushions, then came back and got two of the envelopes. I ran to the telephone, then didn't know who to call. I grabbed a piece of paper to write a note, then decided I didn't have time.

I wished Marty was there. I needed somebody to talk to. Anybody.

And time was going by.

Finally I dropped the fake papers and grabbed up the four envelopes. Carmen was in danger. I'd do exactly what I was told.

I yanked open the door and stepped onto the porch just as Dad's pickup turned into our driveway. I stopped cold. He shouldn't have been there. He couldn't have made the trip to Uncle Gene's. Nobody could drive that fast.

I thought about running, but I just stood there.

Dad hopped out of the pickup. "Sam, are you all right?"

"Yeah." I turned and stepped back into the house.

Dad came inside and shut the door. "I didn't feel like driving all the way out there tonight."

I felt the surge run up my arms. He was lying.

Dad stood with his back to the door. I held the envelopes against my chest, my hands shaking. I backed against the wall. I needed something to hold me up.

"What do you have there?" he asked.

I stared at him. He hadn't gone to Uncle Gene's. Where had he gone? I thought of that faked voice on the phone. He could have made that call from the phone booth at the store.

He started across the room, but stopped half way. He had his hand out in front of him. I couldn't tell if he was reaching for me or the envelopes.

I didn't know what to believe. And I couldn't be wrong right then. Carmen was in trouble, and I was her only hope. Once again, I felt completely alone.

Dad took another step toward me, keeping his hand out in front of him. "What's the matter, Sam?"

I kept looking at his face, trying to read what was behind his eyes. I squeezed the envelopes tighter against my chest.

"What is it, Sam? What's wrong?"

"Noth—" I started. Then, in a crazy half-second, everything got clear. There was no way I could be sure, absolutely sure, of anything. I had to take a chance and do something. And, even with him lying to me, I'd take my chances with Dad.

"The guy called here," I burst out. "He's got Carmen. I'm supposed to bring the papers to the schoolyard right now."

Dad ran across the room and grabbed the phone. "What's Carmen's number?"

I rattled off the numbers and Dad dialed them. I felt fifty pounds lighter. I wasn't alone anymore.

"Melinda?" Dad said into the receiver. "This is Ken Thompson. Is Carmen there? No, I don't need to talk to her. I just want to be sure she's there." A few seconds later, Dad broke into a smile. "Would you do me a favor and keep her with you for the next hour? I'll call back and explain later." He banged down the phone.

"She's there?" I asked.

"It was a bluff," Dad said. "Thank goodness for that." He looked at me. "Do you have Uncle Gene's papers or not?"

"They're right here." I held out the envelopes.

He rushed to the table and started gathering up magazines. "We've got to get something for you to take that looks like those things."

"I have these fakes already." I dropped the envelopes onto the couch and scooped up the papers bags.

"Good," Dad said. "Did he tell you where to put them?"

"By the mailbox."

"I'll slip down there and keep an eye out." He headed for the side door. "Give me two minutes, then go straight down the road. Leave the papers and come right back here and lock the door."

While I waited, I shoved the real papers back under the refrigerator. Then I went out, swinging the bags back and forth so that anybody watching would be sure to see them. I felt like running, but I had to give Dad time to get there.

It's about three hundred yards from my house to the schoolyard. In that distance you go past four houses. Lights were on at each one, but I kept my head turned away. I wanted to get my eyes used to the darkness.

By the time I got to the schoolyard, I could see pretty well. But there was nothing to see. I glanced toward the woodshed, wondering if Marty was inside. I didn't dare go over there.

I set the bags beside the mailbox, then turned and ran all the way home. I locked and bolted the door, then checked the windows again.

After turning off the lights in the living room, I opened a window a few inches. I knelt by the windowsill and peered out into the dark. The only sound I could hear was somebody's dog barking.

I shut that window and went to one by the side door. All I could hear was that same stupid dog.

I was locking the window when I heard footsteps in our driveway, then on our porch. Somebody hammered on the front door.

I dashed to the living room. "Who is it?" I called out. I tried to keep my voice low so that I'd sound like Dad.

"It's the big bad wolf," Marty said. "Let me in."

I slid back the bolt and yanked open the door. "Come on in." As soon as he was inside, I shut the door and locked it again.

"What happened?" he asked. "I saw you come up to the edge of the schoolyard, then turn around and run off."

"Things didn't work out the way we thought."

"I guess not. I sat in that dumb woodshed for an hour, and Carmen didn't even show up."

"The guy called here," I told him. "He said he had Carmen." Marty spun around and started for the door. I grabbed his arm. "Don't worry. She's fine."

"But what—"

"I'll tell you in a second. He called and said he had Carmen. He told me to put the papers by the school mailbox."

"Oh, brother," Marty said. "You did it, didn't you?"

"I would have. But before I left here, Dad came back. I told him what had happened, and he called Carmen's place. It turned out Carmen was still home. So the whole thing was a bluff."

Marty let out a slow whistle. "You scared me for a minute."

"I know."

He turned and looked at me. "But you took the papers down to the mailbox anyway?"

"The fake ones. Dad's down there watching."

"I saw him," Marty said. "Or he saw me. I was walking across the schoolyard, and he came up behind me and put his hand on my shoulder. I jumped about ten feet. He told me to come up here."

"Not exactly the way we planned it."

"I should have known something like this would happen," Marty said. "Mom was making pots and Dad was gone. I was supposed to be in my room doing my homework. I left a note on my bed and sneaked off. They've probably found the note by now." He took a breath and blew it out in a hiss. "And I'm in big-time trouble for nothing."

"Listen," I told him, "it wasn't my dad."

Marty gave me a funny look. "Who said it was?"

"I thought it was him. He told me a bunch of lies, see? And I thought he must be the one. But I was wrong."

"Sometimes you're really dumb," Marty said.

"But it could have been him! All the times worked out, and he was lying about where he went and what he was doing."

Marty shook his head. "Dumb, Sam. Really dumb."

"But it's got to be somebody around here," I said. "And we still don't know—"

Just then the firebell started to clang. Marty threw open the front door, and I heard a woman shout, "Fire!" We ran across the porch and down the steps.

Other people came running from their houses. Up toward the store, a motor roared and tires squealed. "Fire!" a man yelled.

"Let's go," Marty shouted. Looking straight up the road, I

could see the sky lit up. Marty took off running and I came right behind him. We passed a couple of our neighbors.

"It's the old Matson place!" somebody up ahead called.

"Let it burn!" somebody else yelled.

A man ahead of us quit running. A fire at the Matson house wasn't much of an emergency. Nobody had lived there since the mill shut down. Half the windows were gone, and one section of the roof had caved in last winter.

When Marty and I got there, the pumper truck was already parked in front of the house and men were hosing down the trees close by. "Get the backpumps," Mr. Lopez yelled. "Make sure it doesn't spread."

Marty and I grabbed backpumps and ran for the backyard.

A big orange coal shot out into the sky and landed in front of us. Marty rushed forward and pumped water on it. "For once, I didn't miss out," he said.

That made me think about the fire at Uncle Gene's, and I suddenly realized how stupid I'd been. We'd come charging up the road, leaving the house empty and the door unlocked.

I turned toward Marty, but he'd spotted another flame. I didn't waste time going after him. I just slid out of the backpump, let it fall to the ground, and raced away from the fire. "Are you all right, boy?" a man called.

The road was empty. Everybody was at the Matson place. I dashed straight into our yard, then stopped beside the porch. I tried to listen, but all I could hear were the shouts of people back at the fire and the barking of every dog in town.

I tiptoed across the porch, wishing I hadn't pulled down all the shades. The door was open only a crack. I peered through the crack but couldn't see a thing. I reached out with my left hand and eased the door open a few more inches. A couch cushion was on the floor. It hadn't been there when Marty and I left.

I knew that I should get out of there, but I had to know who it was. I pushed the door open a little wider—wide enough to see that the living room was empty. Cushions had been scattered, and one chair was turned over.

I heard a crash from somewhere in the back, probably my bedroom. I took two steps inside and looked down the hall. Just then a figure stepped out of my room and turned in my direction. I was caught there in the open.

The first thing I recognized was the fire chief's hat. "Dr. Vincent?" I said.

"I saw a man run into your house," he said. "I came after him, but he got away."

The biggest surge I'd ever felt shot through my arms. I backed toward the doorway. "Maybe he's out here."

"Wait," Dr. Vincent called. "I want you to see something."

Like an idiot, I stopped. I wasn't really scared. I was in the doorway and he was still fifteen feet away. If he took a step toward me, I'd be off the porch and gone. "What is it?" I asked.

"This." He pulled a black pistol out of his pocket and pointed it at my chest.

"We'd better look for that guy before he gets away," I said.

But Dr. Vincent wasn't buying that. "Get those papers right now," he said.

With the pistol pointing my way, I was too scared to play

any games. I walked straight to the refrigerator and dropped onto the floor. I was dragging out the first envelope when I heard Marty say, "Hi, Dr. Vincent."

I looked up and saw Dr. Vincent pointing his gun toward the front door. "Get in here," he said. "Now!" Then he was running through the door, yelling, "Stop!" I heard his feet pound across the porch and hit the gravel.

I crawled into the living room and slammed the door shut. Then I reached up and slid the bolt into place.

Keeping low in case he fired into the house, I moved over to the telephone. I tried the store first, and the phone rang and rang. Then I tried Carmen's place, but again nobody answered. So Carmen had finally gotten to a fire.

After that, I called the operator and got through to the sheriff's department. When a women answered, I said, "This is Sam Thompson at Alder Creek. We have an emergency here. Fire and kidnapping. The guy who did it is Dr. Vincent." I hung up when she started asking questions.

I crawled back to the refrigerator, got the envelopes, and stuffed them in my shirt. Then I headed for the side door. I was scared to go outside, but I couldn't stay where I was. I'd already seen two houses on fire.

Before I got to the door, Marty was banging on the other side. "Hey, Sam, it's okay."

I unlocked the door and pulled it open. "Is he gone?"

"He ran off," Marty said.

"You all right?"

He smiled and shook his head. "A little shaky, but I guess I'm okay. Dr. Vincent—I can't believe it!"

"Me neither."

"He could have shot me," Marty said. "He had the gun pointed right at me."

"Let's get out of here," I said. "He might change his mind and come back."

We slipped out the side door and moved through the backyard. We crossed over into the Hinshaws' yard. Standing there in the dark, we could see flames shooting into the sky. People were still yelling and dogs were still barking.

"I don't know what's going on," Marty said. "Why would Dr. Vincent—"

"It's crazy," I said. "Maybe he—"

"Duck!" Marty grabbed my shoulder and pulled me to the ground. "Somebody's coming." I could hear the hum of a motor and the crunch of tires on the gravel. We crawled toward the road, then dropped onto our stomachs in the middle of the Hinshaws' ivy. A truck without lights floated past us.

"I'll bet it's him," I said.

The truck's headlights flashed on and the motor roared.

We recognized the taillights right away. "That's his Range Rover!" Marty said.

"He's outa here!" I started feeling better as the taillights got smaller and smaller. "I still don't get it."

"I don't either," Marty said, scrambling to his feet. "But we've got a fire to fight."

We took off running.

Nineteen

"**S**am!"

I stopped running and looked back. Marty ducked his head and dashed away from the road.

"It's all right," I called out. "It's Dad."

Dad came jogging up the road. "You were supposed to stay in the house," he said. "With the door locked."

"It's all over," I said. "It was Dr. Vincent. He was the one. And he just went barreling out of here."

"I saw him," Dad said.

I told Dad about finding Dr. Vincent in the house. Marty stood next to me, but he was turned sideways so that he could see the fire. When I finished, Dad said, "You don't mind very well." But he didn't sound mad.

"I'm sorry," I said. "When we heard the firebell, we sort of forgot everything else."

"I did the same thing," Dad said. "I was afraid it was our house, so I came running up this way. He must have gone to the mailbox right then, found the fake papers, and then gone to our place."

"But why?" I asked. "Why'd he do it?"

"I can't figure it out," Dad said. "I was pretty sure he was the one, but I didn't know why he did it."

Right then I was more interested in other things. "Can we go see the fire?"

"We'd better call the sheriff first."

"I already called him," I said. "And you don't need us." I started edging away. "Please. Can we go?"

He waved us away. "All right. Go. But stay right there with the others. I don't think Vincent will come back but stay close just the same."

Marty and I raced up the road. When we got to the Matson place, most of the people were standing around the pumper truck. But I spotted one person with a backpump patrolling the back side—Carmen. "You guys missed all the excitement," she shouted.

"Not all of it," I said.

Deputy Bates showed up while most people were still at the fire. He talked first to Dad and me, then spent a while with Marty.

While I was watching the fire, I remembered something. On Saturday, when Dr. Vincent had been fussing about my report, I had smelled something that I couldn't place. Now, when it was too late to matter, I realized what it was.

Llama spit. That nasty, sour smell.

If I'd used my head, I could have figured out the whole thing right then. Dr. Vincent had driven up to the trailer and started right in on the reports. He hadn't gone near the corral. That meant that Leonard had gotten him earlier, when he was there in a hood and those big boots.

I'd had my chance to play detective, and I'd muffed it.

Deputy Bates came home with us and slept on our couch. In the morning, after Dad fixed breakfast, the three of us went over to the school. Bates got Mr. Harrison to unlock the storage room so he could use it for an office.

While Bates drove to the store to talk to Mr. and Mrs. Lopez, Dad and I cleared off two tables, then spread Uncle Gene's papers across one of them. "Same old stuff," I said, pawing through the maps and photocopied papers and some hand-drawn sketches that could have been done by a third grader. In one of the envelopes, wrapped in a piece of news-paper, were a bunch of snapshots I hadn't seen before. I was excited at first, but they turned out to be the Polaroid shots Uncle Gene had taken of the marijuana plants. I figured he was keeping them until he got his reward.

"None of it makes any sense," Dad said. "Uncle Gene's had these papers for years, and he showed them to anybody who'd look. If Dr. Vincent wanted to see them, all he had to do was ask."

"He sure wanted these things," I said. I shivered for a second, remembering that pistol pointing at my chest.

Dad pulled up a chair, took a pile of papers, and started through them. He'd glance at each one, then set it aside. "Nothing here I haven't seen before," he muttered.

Carmen looked in the door. "Hi, Sam. Hi, Mr. Thompson."

"Hi, Carmen," I said. "You get my vote for fire chief."

"You're too young to vote," she said. "Too bad." She looked around the room. "What're you doing?"

"Waiting for Deputy Bates mostly," I said. "He's gonna use this room as his office today."

"Can I come in?" she asked after she was already inside. "These are Uncle Gene's papers?"

"That's right," Dad said. "If you see anything valuable, you've got better eyes than I do." He reached for another pile.

Carmen flipped through some photocopied maps, then picked up the Polaroid shots. "What are these?"

"Just what you need," I said. "Blurry pictures of pot plants. They're the ones Uncle Gene took as proof, to be sure he got the reward."

Carmen thumbed through the stack. "I guess it's hard to take good pictures when your hands shake."

Dad sighed and set aside another pile of papers. "These copies are so old they're falling apart."

"Sam," Carmen said, holding out one of the pictures, "what's this?"

I glanced at it. "More blurry pot plants."

"Up in the corner, next to the tree."

I looked closer at the picture. "Is that a tree?" And then I saw what she meant—something silver leaning against the tree trunk.

"I'll get a magnifying glass," Carmen said. She rushed out of the room.

"What is it?" Dad asked.

"Take a look," I said.

Dad held the picture close to his eyes, then moved it back. "I think she's got it," he said, breaking into a smile. "Now it makes sense."

Carmen came running back with the magnifying glass. I reached for it, but she pushed my hand away. "No way," she said. "I get first look." She put the picture on the table and leaned over it, moving the glass up and down. "Yes, yes!" she burst out. "It's his stick!"

She handed me the glass, and I took a careful look. She was right. It was a silver stick. Or, to be more precise, Dr. Vincent's stainless steel walking stick.

I handed the glass to Dad. "I can't believe it. Why would Dr. Vincent be raising marijuana?"

Dad looked at the picture for a minute. "Same reason anybody else does, I guess. Easy money. The kind of stuff he liked doesn't come cheap."

"But why would he take a chance like that?" I asked.

"He probably didn't think there was much risk. Probably nobody's been in that canyon for years. But then Uncle Gene came along and spoiled the whole thing." Dad looked at the picture again. "And even then it was crazy bad luck. Uncle Gene happened to come along when Dr. Vincent was out there." He shook his head and handed Carmen the glass. "He was probably hiding, watching Gene the whole time."

I held up the picture. "So with his bad eyes, Uncle Gene never saw that stick."

"Right," Dad said. "If Dr. Vincent could have gotten rid of the pictures, he would have been free and clear."

Carmen shook her head. "He would have saved himself a lot of trouble if he'd known how bad the pictures were. One fuzzy snapshot with a walking stick up in the corner—that's not much proof."

"Oh, that picture wouldn't put him in jail," Dad said. "But that's not the point."

I looked at him. "It isn't?"

"You know what Dr. Vincent is like. He loves being head of things—the school board, the fire department. If people found out he was growing pot, he'd lose all that."

"That's crazy," I said.

Dad shook his head. "Not really. That's the kind of man he is. He was going to lose everything that mattered to him."

It all made sense. But I didn't like it. I wished it had been somebody rotten like Amos Lawlor who'd done it.

Carmen examined the picture again. "What do you know?" she said. "For once, I was in the middle of things."

Later that morning another deputy showed up with Uncle Gene. Uncle Gene had heard the whole story, but he was still confused. Dad explained everything again, slowly, but Uncle Gene couldn't shake the idea that somebody was after his maps.

"Come on, old timer," Deputy Bates said, "wake up and smell the coffee. Nobody wants your old maps."

"That's how much you know," Uncle Gene said. "I'm gettin' real close."

Bates laughed. "I'll bet."

Uncle Gene's face got redder than usual. "You wait."

"I'll wait, but I won't hold my breath."

Uncle Gene snorted. "Ignorant. Just plain ignorant."

"Look, old timer," Bates said. "I know how you can get

some use outa those papers. You can put 'em in your stove, put some kindling on top, and start a fire." He smacked the table and hooted. "That's all they're good for."

Uncle Gene turned toward Dad. "Let the melonhead laugh. We'll show him, won't we, pard?"

I looked at them both. "Dad?"

Uncle Gene grinned. "That's right, boy. Your daddy knows a good thing when he sees one. Him and me—we'll show these guys."

"Dad?" I said again.

Dad winked at me. "Think about it, Sam. When Uncle Gene finds that mine, we can buy a satellite dish."

Twenty

I didn't get a chance to sort things out until after school. Then I sat down with Carmen and Marty and worked through all the lies Dad had told me. His secret partnership with Uncle Gene explained all but two. And Carmen took care of one of those.

"Big mystery," she said. "He came back last night and said he didn't feel like going all the way to Uncle Gene's. What did you expect him to say—that he was worried sick about his little baby boy?"

"All right," I said.

"Listen," she went on, "I'm glad he was worried. I was on my way out the back door when he called. I hate to think how messed up things might have gotten."

I didn't want to think about might-haves. "What about the first day of fishing season?" I said. "He lied about where he caught his fish. How do you explain that?"

"Everybody lies about fish," Marty said. "I'd give him that one."

But I couldn't leave anything hanging. After Dad and I finished dinner that night, I sat back in my chair and said, "You know those fish you had on the first day of trout season?"

He smiled. "My championship trout?"

"Mine were bigger," I said. "Where did you catch those?"

"A little creek north of Callahan," he said.

"Callahan?"

"I went down there to see a retired lawyer. I was trying to figure a way to give Uncle Gene some money on a regular basis. So I got a lawyer to draw up a big official-looking contract saying Gene got money every month and I got twenty percent of the gold he found. I stopped by the creek on the way home."

"And then you lied about it," I said.

Dad shrugged. "How could I tell you about the fish without telling the rest?"

"That's really tight, Dad," I said. "You've lied to me over and over this spring."

"It wasn't as bad as that," he said. "I just had a little secret, that's all."

"You didn't think you could trust me, did you?"

"Think about it, Sam. Wouldn't you have told Marty? And Carmen?"

I shrugged.

"It was nobody's business. Uncle Gene was close to starving. This was a way to give him grocery money without taking away his pride."

"That part was good," I said.

"And I didn't want anybody else to know."

"I'm not anybody else," I told him. I stopped for a second,

and then the words starting pouring out. "I was scared. I didn't know what was going on. I even thought you might be the one causing the trouble."

Dad laughed and shook his head. "Me—the kidnapper and arsonist? You're kidding."

It made me mad to have him treat the whole thing like a joke. "I'm not kidding," I said. "And it's not funny."

Dad kept laughing. "You actually thought—"

"It's not funny!" I yelled. "I was scared!" And then the dumbest thing happened. There at the kitchen table, after everything was taken care of and everybody was safe, I started to cry. "I was scared," I sobbed. "You kept lying, and I didn't know what to think."

Dad reached over and put his rough hand on top of mine. "I'm sorry, Sam," he said. "I just—"

I looked up then and saw tears in his eyes too. I'm glad nobody had a camera.

I reached up and wiped my eyes. "This is so stupid."

Dad held on to my hand. "Never again," he said. "From now on, it's the truth, the whole truth, and nothing but. Okay?"

"You bet," I said.

We sat there for a long time. Finally Dad said, "Are you all right now?"

I smiled at him and started to say yes. Then I caught myself. It would have been a lie. And we weren't going to lie anymore. "Dad," I said, "I want to talk about Mom sometimes. It's hard, but I want to do it."

He squeezed my hand. "I've done a lousy job there, Sam."

"Me too."

"You want to look at some pictures of your mom?" He pushed his chair back and stood up. "I've got boxes of them."

"Sure."

He hurried toward his room. "I've got a whole bunch that were taken just after you were born. I'm warning you though. You were a funny-looking little baby."

Twenty-one

It's G-Day minus thirteen now. All that stuff seems like a long time ago. Except to Carmen. She's been reading detective stories ever since.

The way things turned out, her detective work didn't matter much. That same morning, Dr. Vincent drove to the sheriff's office and turned himself in. He confessed to everything, but he said he'd been on some medication that had made him crazy. For all I know, it could be true.

At first I hated him—the biggest liar of the bunch. The guy who lectured us on being good citizens and then went out and started a marijuana farm. But then Marty and I got a letter from him. He wanted us to know that he'd never had any bullets in his gun. "I did many things I'm ashamed of," he wrote, "but I would never have harmed you boys." That didn't make me like him, but I was glad to get the letter.

Right now he's in the county jail. He's a prisoner, but he's helping to run their education program. According to Deputy Bates, all the county people love Dr. Vincent. So do the prisoners. He's been helping them with their legal problems and setting up study groups. I guess he'd be elected mayor of the jail, if they had one.

I still hate the things he did. And I don't understand why he did them. But I miss him in a way. I sometimes wish he could show up at school again with a bird's nest or a fossil to show us.

After my talk with Dad, I quit caring about who was lying and who wasn't. As long as I couldn't tell good lies from bad lies, I didn't want any part of it.

At first I was excited about being able to know the truth, but it's not that simple. I heard those people tell lies, and then I saw the same people run to help somebody in trouble. Which part is the real truth?

I like Marty's way. He says he believes everybody, even liars.

Stopping the whole business wasn't as hard as I thought. Whenever I got a surge up my arms, I just closed my eyes for a second and took a deep breath. And the surges quit coming so often.

I still get one now and then, but it's like a mosquito bite. It bothers for a minute, but if you ignore it, it goes away.

Right now, though, I have other problems—like graduation. Marty and I know what we'd like. In the Yreka newspaper, he found an article about an eighth-grade class taking a graduation trip to Paris. That sounded good to us. Now all we need is five thousand bucks.

What we'll probably get is punch and cookies. Mr. Harrison says we can have a regular graduation ceremony if we want. Marty thought it would be funny to wear black caps and gowns and to come marching in. But the more we talked about it, the stupider it sounded.

Carmen says we should have a ceremony. She says she's going to have one next year, all by herself, if she's still living here by then.

I hope she's still here. I hate to think what Alder Creek would be like without her.

So I guess that's about it. We're back to SOT and MOTSOT, especially after the Lawlors left town last week. Right after that, people started missing stuff from their toolsheds. So Mr. Lawlor must have taken a lot of souvenirs with him.

Even Uncle Gene is gone—for a while. He had Leonard at the store yesterday, loading him with supplies. Uncle Gene had finally gotten his hundred dollars reward from the sheriff, and he still had the money from the Reno trip. That bought more groceries than Leonard wanted to carry.

"I'm headin' further west this time," Uncle Gene told me. "And I'm feelin' real lucky. I figger the Barkley Mine is sittin' out there just waitin' for me."

I hope he's right. That's the only way I can think of for Marty and me to get that trip to Paris.

About the author

P. J. Petersen was born in Santa Rosa, California, and grew up on a prune farm in Sonoma County. He attended Stanford University and holds the doctorate in English from the University of New Mexico. He lives with his family in Redding, California, and teaches at Shasta College.

Among his many books for children and young adults are two American Library Association Best Books for Young Adults, *Would You Settle for Improbable?* and *Nobody Else Can Walk It for You*.

The idea for *Liars* came to Mr. Petersen, he says, "After I, a total skeptic, discovered I had the ability to 'dowse'—that is, to detect water underground. This discovery started me thinking about undiscovered and unrecognized powers."